A loud shriek rang out upstairs and Elizabeth jumped to her feet, her heart pounding. "What—what—was th-that?"

"I don't know!" Amy said, clutching the wool afghan blanket on her lap.

"No! Stay away!" the voice screeched.

"It's one of the kids!" Amy said, getting up quickly. "I thought it was in the movie or—"

"That's Juliana!" Elizabeth realized. "She's having a nightmare!" She and Amy dashed into the hallway and flew up the stairs, heading straight for Juliana's bedroom. Elizabeth ran in and flipped on the overhead light.

Juliana was thrashing from side to side in her bed, the sheets and blanket a twisted tangle around her. "No! No, you can't!" she yelled.

Elizabeth ran to Juliana's side and touched her shoulder, shaking her gently. "Juliana, wake up. Wake up, it's OK!"

Juliana blinked her eyes a few times and looked at Elizabeth. "Elizabeth!" she cried. "It was—it was her!" She burst into tears.

"Her?" Elizabeth suddenly remembered Juliana telling her about the monster girl, who was trying to "get" her. Apparently the same girl was still frightening Juliana in her dreams. But why?

SWEET VALLEY TWINS

Too Scared to Sleep

Written by
Jamie Suzanne

Created by
FRANCINE PASCAL

BANTAM BOOKS
NEW YORK · TORONTO · LONDON · SYDNEY · AUCKLAND

TOO SCARED TO SLEEP
A BANTAM BOOK : 0 553 50338 3

Originally published in USA by Bantam Books

First publication in Great Britain

PRINTING HISTORY
Bantam edition published 1997

The trademarks "Sweet Valley" and "Sweet Valley Twins"
are owned by Francine Pascal and are used under license by
Bantam Books and Transworld Publishers Ltd.

Conceived by Francine Pascal

Produced by Daniel Weiss Associates, Inc,
33 West 17th Street, New York, NY 10011

Cover photo by Oliver Hunter

Bantam Books are published by Transworld Publishers Ltd,
61–63 Uxbridge Road, London W5 5SA,
in Australia by Transworld Publishers (Australia) Pty Ltd,
15–25 Helles Avenue, Moorebank, NSW 2170,
and in New Zealand by Transworld Publishers (NZ) Ltd,
3 William Pickering Drive, Albany, Auckland.

Printed and bound in Great Britain by
Cox & Wyman Ltd, Reading, Berkshire.

One

The girl walks around and around the circular stairs, winding her way up until she reaches the very top of the house, the third floor. Then she pushes open a door and steps out onto the widow's walk. Bright moonlight reflects off the white balcony, and the night's gentle breeze ruffles her nightgown.

She gazes up at the dark starry sky and looks out over the twinkling lights of the small town. Sweet Valley. It looks so innocent and quiet at night.

She can smell the ocean nearby. She takes a few steps toward the balcony railing, the wood floor creaking beneath her. When she puts her hand on the railing, cracking paint flutters over the edge, drifting three stories down and landing on the overgrown bushes in front of the house.

Good, she thinks. Nobody will ever live here for long—not as shabby as the place is.

She doesn't want anyone to live in the house. Not ever.

But now some people have come to stay. A big family, with lots of little kids making noise all the time, running around, playing and yelling, having fun.

They have moved in so easily, as if this were their house. As if they belong here. They don't. And she is going to make sure they don't stay.

"No child will ever sleep safely in this house again," she says into the quiet, deserted darkness. *"Ever!"*

"Elizabeth! Wait up!"

Elizabeth Wakefield turned around, slowly coasting at the top of the long hill she had just climbed on her bike. "Come on, Jessica. You can make it!" she called back, trying to encourage her twin. She and Jessica were on their way to the beach to meet some friends for a Saturday morning game of volleyball.

Jessica slowly rode up beside her, panting loudly. "No wonder we don't usually come to the beach this way. It's like climbing the Alps or something!"

Elizabeth laughed, shaking her head. "It's not quite as bad as the Alps. But it is pretty steep. Can you imagine having to do this every day?"

"No. No, I think I'd definitely move," Jessica said. "Like the Sullivans did." She glanced up a long driveway to a white mansion on the hill above them.

"I thought they moved because the house was haunted," Elizabeth said. "Isn't a ghost supposed to live there now?"

She knew that after the Sullivans moved out, the

house had stood abandoned for years—as long as she could remember, nobody had lived in it.

Every year during Halloween it was a Sweet Valley tradition to run past the spooky Sullivan house, shrieking at the top of your lungs. Elizabeth didn't know who'd started the tradition—but she knew that every time she came past the house after dark on Halloween, she was scared half to death by the plastic ghosts and goblins neighbors hung from the bushes and trees.

"I wouldn't live up here if you paid me—hey, wait a second." Jessica jammed the brakes on her bike, and her tires squeaked. "Look!" She pointed up the driveway.

Elizabeth shielded her eyes from the sun and followed Jessica's gaze. "What is that? A truck?" She could just make out the back end of a large squarish vehicle.

"Let's go see!" Jessica said excitedly.

"I don't know, Jessica—this is private property," Elizabeth said, slowly following her sister up the curving driveway.

"You're such a chicken! Like we're going to see a truck here for the first time and just, like, *ride by*," Jessica said. "We've got to check it out. Even if this place is a little creepy." She changed gears and started pedaling harder.

Elizabeth frowned, but she followed Jessica anyway. It was typical for her sister to barge in and investigate something without thinking. Elizabeth preferred to go more slowly—she didn't mind taking risks, but only when she had time to think them through.

That wasn't the only difference between Elizabeth and Jessica. Even though they were identical twins, and both had blond hair, blue-green eyes, and the same dimple in their left cheek, they were completely different on the inside. Jessica was impulsive; Elizabeth was logical—at least usually, she thought with a smile. At school Jessica hung out with her friends in the Unicorn Club, a group of girls who considered themselves the prettiest and most popular around. She preferred socializing to studying.

Elizabeth was more serious and thoughtful than her twin. Her favorite activities included having long talks with her friends, writing for the school newspaper, and reading a good mystery.

The twins even wore their hair in different styles: Elizabeth tied hers back in a ponytail or held it back with barrettes, while Jessica wore hers long and loose. And they dressed like total opposites, too— Jessica wore all the latest trends, while Elizabeth preferred simpler, more comfortable clothes. But that didn't stop Jessica from borrowing outfits from Elizabeth whenever she felt like it.

Of course, all their differences didn't really matter much to Elizabeth. She still thought of Jessica as her best friend in the world.

Elizabeth kept her eyes on the old Sullivan house as she rode her bike beside Jessica. As they got closer she saw two small children run out onto the wide porch. "Did you just see what I saw?" she asked.

"Was that a couple of kids?" Jessica asked her sister. "I can't believe it."

"Look!" Elizabeth pointed to the large truck. Mid-Coast Moving was painted in large letters on the side, and two men were walking out of it, carrying a large red couch. "Somebody's moving in!"

"No *way*," Jessica said. "Who would?"

"More to the point, *why* would they?" Elizabeth added. "Why would anyone want to live in this creepy old—"

A burst of shrieking laughter interrupted her as several young children wheeled around the corner of the moving truck, chasing each other at top speed.

"There must be ten kids in this family," Jessica observed.

"No wonder they want this house—it's one of the biggest in town!" Elizabeth commented. She watched a boy who looked like he was about two years old playing with a plastic truck on the lawn.

"Kids! Stay out of the way of the movers!" A woman rushed out of the house, wearing a red college sweatshirt and blue jeans. Her hair was covered with a bandanna, and she had on running sneakers. "Careful with that couch—it's an antique!" she shouted, running over to the movers, who had set one end of the couch on the driveway. She dashed toward the truck, waving her hands in the air. She headed right for the twins, who were perched on their bikes at the end of the sidewalk. "Whoa!" she exclaimed, stopping just short of Jessica.

"Watch where you're going!" Jessica said, jumping off her bike before the woman could knock it over. "Somebody might get hurt!"

"What she means is, sorry we're in your way," Elizabeth hastened to add, with an apologetic look.

"No, I'm the one who's sorry! Hello!" the woman replied, sounding a bit frazzled. She took a step backward and tucked a loose strand of dark brown hair back under her bandanna. "I apologize—things are so hectic around here, I've completely forgotten my manners. I'm Mrs. Riccoli." She smiled at the twins.

"I'm Jessica, and this is Elizabeth. Wakefield, that is," Jessica added. "We were on our way to the beach when we saw the moving truck—we had to see who was moving in!"

"Well, so far just me and my kids!" Mrs. Riccoli pointed to each of them one by one. "That's Olivia, Andrew, Gretchen, Juliana, and . . . oh, where has Nate gone to now?"

Elizabeth saw the youngest boy peering at her from underneath the other side of the moving truck. "There he is!" she cried.

"Nate, get away from there!" Mrs. Riccoli scolded. "Oh. This has been the longest day of my life, and it's only ten-thirty!" She hurried over to grab Nate and picked him up in her arms.

"Is there anything we can do to help?" Elizabeth offered. She'd never seen anyone so busy before—

with so much to look after at once! "Maybe we could watch the kids for a few minutes, give you a chance to catch your breath or have a cup of coffee . . ."

Jessica cleared her throat.

Elizabeth glanced at her. "Do you have a scratchy throat, Jess?" she asked.

Jessica sighed. "No. It's just that . . ." She turned to Mrs. Riccoli. "Of course, we'd *love* to help," she said. "But the thing *is*, Elizabeth, that we really do have to get going, because people are *waiting* for us and we don't want to be late and make them wait and all."

Elizabeth frowned at her. Now she knew what her sister had been trying to say. She didn't want to help. *Typical Jessica*, Elizabeth thought. Jessica was the last person to pitch in and do something difficult, like help somebody move. Especially when it meant getting dirt on her brand-new purple sweatshirt or crowding her already-full-of-social-events weekend schedule. "Well, we don't have to leave right this second," Elizabeth told Mrs. Riccoli. "Maybe we could—"

"Elizabeth, we're supposed to be there in ten minutes," Jessica argued, tapping her sneaker against the pavement.

"Oh, don't be late on my account!" Mrs. Riccoli said, setting down Nate. The little boy clung to her leg, hiding from Elizabeth. "I'm sure things will calm down here in a little bit. As soon as the truck's unloaded and we can start unpacking. You know, I think I hate unpacking even more than I hate packing!"

"Where did you move from?" Elizabeth asked.

"Sacramento. Andrew, stop that!" she called to her older son, who was chasing a brown-haired girl around the yard, trying to put a large empty cardboard box over her head. At that moment Nate took off, wandering back to the moving truck.

Mrs. Riccoli sighed, shaking her head. "You know, this might be the perfect time to ask you two if you can recommend some good baby-sitters in town! In fact, maybe you're interested? My husband's not going to be moving here for another few months, and I'll need some help."

"A lot of help, it looks like," Elizabeth said, smiling as Andrew captured the little brown-haired girl with the box and she started yelling. "You know, we could baby-sit. If you give us your phone number, we can pass it on to our friends, too."

"Yeah—we have lots of friends," Jessica said. "And some of them baby-sit, like, constantly."

Elizabeth gave her sister a funny look. She didn't know who Jessica was talking about—her friends were usually too busy shopping and throwing parties to baby-sit. And Jessica's best friend, Lila Fowler, was too rich to even consider working on anything but her suntan.

"That would be great. Here's my number." Mrs. Riccoli took a pencil from her back pocket and tore the corner off a map she was carrying, scribbling down the phone number. "If you or any of your friends want to make some money, give me a call!

Now, I'd better get back to—oh, no, Nate, you can't *sit* on the couch while they carry it!" She ran off to intercept the movers as they struggled to get the couch up the front steps.

"Good luck, Mrs. Riccoli!" Elizabeth called as she and Jessica climbed onto their bikes.

"She'll need it," Jessica agreed, coasting down the driveway. "Isn't that house supposed to be haunted?"

Elizabeth laughed. She pointed over her shoulder at the kids, who were playing hide-and-seek in the bushes in front of the house. "Does it *look* haunted?"

"Well . . . not exactly," Jessica said. "But I wouldn't live there."

"Good thing because with all those kids, the Riccolis don't have any extra room for you!" Elizabeth teased, sprinting down the driveway ahead of her.

"Awesome tiebreaker game. Truly awesome," Winston Egbert said. "Almost as awesome as this sundae's going to be." He grinned as Joe Carrey, the new manager at Casey's Ice Cream Parlor, set a huge dish of chocolate chip ice cream with hot fudge in front of him.

"We aim to please," Joe said. "Anything else I can get you guys?" He looked around the booth at Todd Wilkins, Jessica, Elizabeth, and Amy Sutton, one of Elizabeth's best friends.

Elizabeth shook her head. "I think this banana split will hold me for the next . . . three weeks or so, thanks.

"Yeah, right. You'll be back here tomorrow, just like the rest of us," Todd teased her.

Elizabeth blushed. Todd was her sort of boyfriend, and she tended to blush when he teased her. "OK, OK. You're probably right." She smiled shyly at Todd.

"I know *I* will." Jessica dug up a spoonful of hot butterscotch from the bottom of her sundae glass.

Joe laughed. "Well, good. And you can pay me whenever you're ready." He placed a small slip of paper on the table, smiled, and walked away.

Jessica turned to Elizabeth. "You have a couple of dollars I can borrow, don't you? To pay for this?"

Elizabeth practically dropped her spoon. "Me? Pay for you?" She'd been lending Jessica money practically since the day they were born. And Jessica owed her at least *ten* sundaes. "But Jessica, I thought you were paying for me," she protested.

"Why would you think that?" Jessica asked, looking as if Elizabeth had just suggested that she fly to the moon and back before dinner.

"Because I paid the last time. And the time before that, and the time before that, and—"

"OK, so I owe you a couple of sundaes," Jessica said defensively. "You don't have to make a federal case out of it."

"Actually, that might not be a bad idea," Winston said. "Get a good lawyer, take it to the Supreme Court. Sue her, Elizabeth, for everything she's got!" He pounded his fist against the table, hitting a spoon and sending it flying. The spoon landed right on an older man who was sitting in the booth behind them.

"Pardon me, excuse me," Winston said, looking sheepish.

"What do you think you're doing, young man? This isn't a playground!" the man complained, wiping a glob of hot fudge off his bald head.

"Flying spoons are a big problem here at Casey's—didn't you see the warning sign when you came in?" Winston replied, handing him a fresh napkin.

The man glared at Winston and turned back around.

"You win admirers wherever you go, don't you, Winston?" Amy joked. "You're lucky he isn't going to sue *you*."

"It was an accident! You're all witnesses! I have nothing to hide. But what do you think of my plan, Elizabeth?" Winston asked. "I mean, if you're not involved in a lawsuit these days, you're *nobody*."

"You can't sue me!" Jessica warned her. "I'm your sister."

"Sure, she can. Didn't you hear about those triplets in Los Angeles suing each other because they all want to marry the same guy?" Amy asked.

Winston nodded. "Debbie, Donna, and Darlene. And if triplets can sue each other, *twins* definitely can."

"Well, even if I did sue Jessica, I wouldn't get anything. She doesn't have any money," Elizabeth grumbled. And now, thanks to Jessica, neither did *she* anymore.

"Sorry," Jessica said meekly, shrugging. "I told

Mom and Dad to give me the raise *first*, then start worrying about my grades. But did they listen?" She threw up her hands. "No!"

"I'd help you guys out, but I don't have any extra money on me," Amy said.

"Neither do I," Todd added. "I'm down to my last three bucks."

"And after the incredibly huge tip I leave for *Joe*," Winston said loudly as the manager came back toward their table, "I'll be broke for years!"

"There's no need to go broke over me," Joe said, shaking his head at Winston.

"Too late," Jessica grumbled, slumping down in her seat.

You can say that again, Elizabeth thought. Jessica had gone broke in the second grade, and from then on it was all downhill! She looked up at Joe and tried to smile—there was no point taking her bad mood out on him.

"Everything OK?" Joe asked. "How are the sundaes?"

"Great. Except . . ." Elizabeth paused. How was she going to put this? "Except . . . this is really awful, Joe, but we can't exactly pay for all of them."

"Oh." Joe nodded. "You guys weren't kidding about going broke, were you? Well, it's no problem."

"It's not? You mean . . . I can eat here free tomorrow, too?" Winston joked. "Cool!"

"I don't know if I can afford that," Joe said. "But I'd be happy to run a little tab for you."

"That would be great." Jessica smiled sweetly. "Thanks!"

Joe shrugged. "I can hold the bill for a few days. Just stop by with the money when you're ready, and we'll settle up. I'll call it the Super Sundae Layaway Plan," he offered. "Sound good?"

Jessica put her hand on his arm. "Joe, you're *such* a lifesaver. And we promise we'll pay you back just as soon as—"

"No, Jessica. We can't!" Elizabeth cut in.

"We can't?" She looked at Elizabeth with wide eyes. "Hold on. You're not going to say we should hang out here and work as dishwashers all night or something just to pay for—"

"No," Elizabeth interrupted her again. "Listen, Joe, that's a really, really generous offer, and it's totally nice of you. But the thing is, we won't have any more money for another week. And I can't make you wait until then for us to pay!" Elizabeth put her hand in her pocket, hoping she might surprise herself by finding some loose change—at least then she could give Joe something. "Maybe I have a couple of quarters I forgot about—let me check."

But all she pulled out was the small scrap of paper that Mrs. Riccoli had jotted down her phone number on. *Wait a second*, she thought with a flicker of excitement. *This is it! The answer to our problems!*

A smile curled up the corners of her mouth as she turned to Joe. "Actually, if you could give me and Jessica credit—just for a couple of days? I know we'll be able to pay you what we owe."

"Consider it done. Come see me when you're ready." Joe took money from Amy, Winston, and Todd and left the table.

Jessica fixed Elizabeth with a look. "OK, Ms. Moneybags. Ten seconds ago we were both broke. So how are we going to pay back Joe in a couple of days?"

"Elizabeth's going to rob the ATM machine over by the Peppy Pretzel," Winston said. "But don't tell us about it, Elizabeth—we don't want to be accessories to the crime!"

"I'm not going to rob anything," Elizabeth said, laughing. "I'm starting a new business. And if you guys want in on it, you'd better say so now!"

"A new business?" Jessica asked, looking confused.

Elizabeth unfolded the piece of map and held it in front of her sister's face. "We're starting a new baby-sitting service. For Mrs. Riccoli."

"We?" Jessica said. "As in . . . you and me? Baby-sitting?"

"Who's Mrs. Broccoli?" Winston asked.

"It's Mrs. Riccoli," Elizabeth corrected him.

"OK, but I still don't know who she is," Winston said.

"Me neither," Amy said.

"She's a woman we met this morning," Elizabeth explained. The setup was perfect—why hadn't she thought of it before? "She has five kids, and they just moved into the big old Sullivan mansion—"

Todd started making eerie whistling noises, sounding like an evil spirit in a horror movie.

Elizabeth laughed. "Quit it! That house isn't any more haunted than the mall. Not now! You should see those kids—they're all really cute. And Mrs. Riccoli totally has her hands full, and she practically begged us to find baby-sitters for her. They just got to town, so she doesn't *know* anyone else."

"In other words, if we want this job, we've got it?" Amy asked.

Elizabeth nodded. "Definitely. And she's going to need a lot of help. Which means—"

"A lot of money!" Jessica said. She sat up straight in the booth, her eyes shining.

"Exactly," Elizabeth said. "And if we play our cards right, we can keep the Riccoli family all to ourselves. Between the five of us we should be able to handle most of their baby-sitting needs."

"OK," Jessica said, "but that means splitting the money five ways." She frowned. "I don't know if that's going to be enough for me."

First she doesn't have any money—and then she wants to hog it all! Elizabeth thought. "We'll *share* the work," she explained to her sister. She paused for a minute to think things over. Five baby-sitters . . . and five kids . . . actually, it would work out pretty nicely. They could each earn a certain amount per week. "For instance," she suggested, "you and I can baby-sit one night, Jessica. And Todd and Winston the next . . . then me and Amy . . . like that! We'll need to double up to look after them all. I'm sure we'll make plenty of money. If we don't, we can always work for other families, too." She glanced at Jessica, whose eyes were glazed over, as if she were concentrating very hard on something.

"We could make a *ton* of money doing this," Jessica murmured happily.

"OK, but how are all these people going to find out about us?" Winston asked.

"Easy," Elizabeth said. "We'll make a couple of signs and put them on the bulletin board at the supermarket."

Jessica nodded. "Big signs. Really big signs they can't miss."

"That's a great idea," Amy said. "You know, this works out perfectly for me. I could use some extra spending money. I've really been wanting a portable CD player."

"And I could use some new Rollerblades," Todd mused.

"Well, get in line. I need *everything*!" Jessica declared. "A CD player, Rollerblades, *and* a new plaid backpack, a corduroy coat—brown, probably, and lots of other things in brown because that's the major color for the season, you know, and—does anyone have a pen?"

"Brown, you say." Winston wiggled his eyebrows. "Good. I've got my eye on this brown miniskirt. I think it'll look *totally* hot on me."

"Whatever you say." Elizabeth laughed. "Just get

ready to start making money! And then, maybe, you can pay for my sundae next time?" she said, turning to Jessica.

Jessica was crouched over a clean napkin, furiously writing things she wanted to buy. "Can somebody grab me another napkin?" she asked without looking up.

"Then again . . . maybe not," Elizabeth said, smiling wryly at Amy.

Two

◇

Late Saturday afternoon Winston entered a small office building, headed up the stairs, and stopped in the hallway outside Mr. Pagnowski's office. Then, glancing over his shoulder, he quickly turned the knob and slipped inside. It was very important that nobody see him. And even more important that nobody see what he was carrying. He set the large, bulky case down on the floor and wiped his brow. Not only did he have a major secret, it was a very, very *heavy* secret.

"Good afternoon, Mr. Egbert." Mr. Pagnowski looked up from some papers he was examining on his desk. He was about fifty years old and had brown hair, a mustache, and tiny reading glasses. "Are you ready?"

"Hi, Mr. Pagnowski." Winston smiled nervously. "I hope so."

"Well, let's see." Mr. Pagnowski patted the chair next to him, and Winston sat down, opening the case. "And how has your practicing been going?"

"Fine, I guess." Winston shrugged.

"We will know soon enough, eh?" Mr. Pagnowski chuckled.

"That's the problem," Winston said, lifting the instrument out of its case and slipping the wide straps over his shoulders.

"Don't worry, Winston. You always think you're doing terribly when you are actually making excellent progress. In fact, we will have you playing polkas for your mother in no time," Mr. Pagnowski predicted, adjusting his eyeglasses.

Great! Winston thought, stifling a sigh. He didn't *want* to learn how to play a polka. And he definitely didn't want to spend his Saturday afternoons in Mr. Pagnowski's stuffy office, playing the accordion. The accordion had to be the weirdest, most old-fashioned instrument on the planet. Winston didn't know anybody his age who played it. For that matter, he didn't know anyone who even knew what an accordion looked like! *Maybe I can carry it around and tell people it's a funky new kind of synthesizer,* Winston thought as he glanced down at the accordion. *Yeah, right.*

Not that Winston had anything against the instrument. It was interesting, in its own way. And it probably came in handy at parties for people over the age of fifty or in other countries, where it was part of the culture and people considered it a cool thing to know how to play. But Winston would much rather be taking drum lessons with Mr. Pagnowski and practicing for his big solo at the school concert, the one where he'd blow everyone away, his hands moving at the speed of light, cymbals crashing. . . .

Instead he was taking accordion lessons so he could play a polka at his mom's second cousin's daughter's wedding in a month. His mother insisted on it; she loved polkas, and she thought it would be wonderful if Winston became the polka player for the Egberts. *What's she going to do?* Winston wondered. *Fly me around the country to all the family events?*

"All right, then. All set?" Mr. Pagnowski asked, shuffling a few sheets of music and sitting in a folding chair beside Winston. He placed the music on the stand in front of Winston.

"I guess so," Winston said, trying to muster a smile. For some reason, he completely lost his sense of humor whenever he was sitting with a twenty-pound accordion on his lap, strapped onto him like a life preserver.

"Then we will start with a few warming-up exercises," Mr. Pagnowski said.

Winston nodded. He squeezed the accordion in and out, pressing the chord buttons with his left hand as he played the scale on the keys with his right hand.

"Something a little more difficult now," Mr. Pagnowski said. "Do you remember what we went over last time?"

Winston nodded. How could he forget? Mr. Pagnowski had made him play the same sequence at least fifty times, until he played it perfectly. Winston began playing the short warm-up, focusing as hard as he could, trying to get each chord right.

Suddenly the office door flew open, the doorknob banging against the wall. "Sorry I'm late, Mr. Pag . . . Egghead?"

Winston looked up from the accordion. Charlie Cashman was standing in the doorway, carrying a guitar case, a wide smirk on his face. Winston let all the air out of the accordion and it bleated, like a lost sheep.

Charlie was an eighth-grader and one of the meanest kids at Winston's school, if not *the* meanest. He lived to make fun of people. And here was Winston, with the nerdiest instrument on the planet strapped to his chest. He might as well be wearing a banner saying, Taunt Me! Make Fun of Me! Please!

"You are not late, Mr. Cashman—you are an hour early," Mr. Pagnowski said.

Of course, bullies aren't always known for keeping time, Winston thought. *They're too busy harassing people.*

"Then I guess I'll just have to wait." Charlie set his guitar case on the floor and sat on the piano bench, facing them. "Oh, go ahead—don't mind me!" he said, grinning at Winston.

"Mrs. Riccoli? This is Elizabeth Wakefield. We met earlier today, when you were moving in?" Elizabeth was sitting on the couch in her living room Saturday afternoon. She and Jessica were about to watch a movie they had rented, but first Elizabeth wanted to talk to Mrs. Riccoli. "Remember me and my sister, Jessica?"

"Oh, of course I remember," Mrs. Riccoli said. "Hello, Elizabeth. How are you?"

"I'm fine," Elizabeth replied. "How's the move going?"

"Ugh," Mrs. Riccoli groaned. "Have you ever tried to get a seven-year-old to unpack?"

"No, but I bet it's pretty hard," Elizabeth said. "Actually, that's why I'm calling. You know how you asked Jessica and me if we knew any baby-sitters in town, and I told you we'd think about it?"

"Of course," Mrs. Riccoli said warmly. "And I hope you're calling with good news for me!"

"I am. Jessica and I talked about it, and we decided that we'd really love to help you out anytime. And we have three friends who want to baby-sit for you, too," Elizabeth offered.

"That's terrific! Oh, I'm so relieved." Mrs. Riccoli sighed. "I didn't know what I was going to do."

"Well, let us help you figure it out," Elizabeth said. "When and how often will you need us to work?"

"Here's the situation," Mrs. Riccoli said. "I'm a professor at Sweet Valley University. For now I've arranged my schedule so that I teach late afternoon and early evening classes. That way I can be home for Nate and Juliana during the day and be here when the other kids get back from school. So the times of day I would need you are, say, between four and eight, perhaps a bit later on some nights, so I can meet with students. I think I told you that my husband won't be moving up from Sacramento for a few months yet. So there will be plenty of work for you and your friends. Plenty!" Mrs. Riccoli laughed. "In fact, you might want to find five *more* friends to help."

"Oh, I'm sure we can handle it," Elizabeth said, trying to sound confident. She didn't want Mrs. Riccoli to hire anyone else—or to worry that they couldn't take care of the kids. "So what does your schedule look like this week?"

"Well, I start teaching on Monday," Mrs. Riccoli said. "So maybe you and your sister could come over at around . . . oh, let's see . . . my Monday, Wednesday, Friday class isn't until six-forty, so . . ."

"We could come over at six," Elizabeth suggested.

"Perfect," Mrs. Riccoli said. "Thanks so much!"

"No problem," Elizabeth said. "See you then!" She hung up the phone and lay back on the couch with a smile. She actually had a new job! It was so exciting.

Jessica walked into the living room, carrying a big bowl of popcorn. She perched on the arm of the couch next to Elizabeth's feet. "Well? How did it go?" She took a handful of popcorn.

"Great. We're actually starting on Monday," Elizabeth told her, holding out her hand for some popcorn.

Jessica passed her the bowl. "Cool. So how much are we going to get paid?"

Elizabeth ate a piece of popcorn, thinking about Mrs. Riccoli and all she had to handle. If she didn't need the money, she'd almost be willing to work for free, just to help her out. "Oh, I don't know. Probably the going rate. I guess we can talk about it when we get there."

"Elizabeth!" Jessica tossed a piece of popcorn at her. "You're supposed to agree to that stuff first, before we agree to show up. It's called negotiating!"

"And we're what's called being broke," Elizabeth said, throwing the popcorn back at her. "We'll take whatever she offers!"

"Humph." Jessica frowned. "Well, at first, maybe. But after a few weeks, I'm asking for a raise!"

Winston flipped the latch on his accordion case closed and stood up. Finally his lesson was over. He couldn't wait to escape. Charlie had sat and stared at him throughout his entire lesson, which hadn't exactly helped his technique. Between Mr. Pagnowski criticizing his playing and Charlie snickering when he hit the wrong notes, Winston was ready to tell his mother to forget about the polka—no family wedding was worth this much pain and suffering! They could call off the wedding or elope as far as he was concerned. What was so wrong with hiring a disc jockey, anyway?

Winston grabbed his jacket and his sheet music. He was hurrying because he didn't want to stick around long enough for Charlie to say anything to him.

"Good-bye, Mr. Pagnowski," Winston said, opening the door.

"See you next week, Mr. Egbert," his teacher replied. "Don't forget—you have ten fingers."

Winston glanced at his hands. "Uh-huh." He didn't understand what Mr. Pagnowski was driving at, but he couldn't argue that point.

"To be an accordion player, you need to use all ten. Today you forgot a few, eh?" Mr. Pagnowski laughed. "No matter. We will get you to use all of them next week."

"Okay, thanks." Winston only wanted to escape before Charlie made a joke about how he was all thumbs. He walked into the hallway. He had taken two steps toward the stairs when he felt a hand on his shoulder.

Winston kept walking, not even bothering to turn around. He didn't feel like dealing with Mr. Pagnowski for another second. "I know, I know, I promise to use all my fingers and—"

Winston broke off as the fingers tightened on his shoulder. A feeling of dread bubbled up inside him, and slowly he turned around. Mr. Pagnowski had gotten a lot shorter all of a sudden—and a lot meaner looking.

"Good. Practice a lot. Because I think we could use a polka number at our next pep rally!" Charlie replied with a wicked grin.

Winston set his heavy case on the floor. "I—I think Mr. Pagnowski is . . . er . . . waiting for you," he stammered.

"He had to make a phone call," Charlie said in a

superior voice. "Which is kind of a coincidence, because I was just thinking of making a few phone calls myself."

Phone calls? About what? "Really?" Winston squeaked.

"Sure! I mean, you can't expect me to keep the exciting news all to myself, can you?" Charlie smiled. "Winston Egbert is becoming a master polka player. I'm sure everyone at school is going to love knowing that you've taken up the geek instrument of all time, the instrument that was *invented* for nerds. In fact, maybe you can even get a gig at somebody's grandparents' golden anniversary party!" He laughed.

Charlie was going to blab his secret to the whole school, Winston suddenly realized. He didn't stand a chance. *Unless, of course, I plead ignorance, which usually works on Charlie.* "You're . . . you're not actually going to tell anyone about this, are you?" Winston asked, looking anxiously at Charlie.

"Oh, no. I'm not going to tell anyone." Charlie shook his head.

Winston heaved a sigh of relief. Maybe Charlie wasn't the monster he thought he was. "You know, Charlie," Winston began, "I always said a person could rely on you—"

"I'm going to tell *everyone*!" Charlie proudly announced, smiling gleefully at the prospect.

"Ev-everyone?" Winston stammered. "Like . . . more than five people?"

"I wonder if I can take out a page in the newspaper. Of course, in my experience word of mouth is always the best way to go. I tell a few friends, they tell a few friends . . . it'll be all over school by lunchtime, Monday."

Winston pictured himself walking into the cafeteria and a chorus of laughter breaking out. He'd sit by himself, in the corner, with his accordion. Just when his social life was actually getting halfway decent! "Please, Charlie. Don't tell anyone," Winston begged.

"Ha! Like I won't!" Charlie scoffed. "What are you going to do, stop me?"

"I'll do anything if you keep your mouth shut about this," Winston said. "Just . . . pretend you never saw me! I'll make it worth your while. I'll . . . do your homework for a month. I'll buy you a new guitar. I'll—"

"Well, maybe we *could* make some kind of a deal," Charlie said slowly. "Only there has to be something good in it for me, because this is *way* too good to just forget about."

Winston bit his lip, thinking desperately. What could he do to make Charlie forget all about his little secret? "I know!" he suddenly cried. "I won't tell anyone you're taking guitar lessons!"

Charlie raised one eyebrow. "And I'm real concerned about that. Girls only go wild over guitar players. Accordion players, on the other hand . . . now, which girl exactly were you planning on asking to the next dance? Maybe I'll let her be the first to know you have your own lounge act."

Winston frantically tried to think of something he

could offer to Charlie to keep him from blabbing. His comic book collection . . . no, too valuable. His favorite L.A. Kings jacket . . . no, too small. His head on a platter . . . no, too disgusting. "Charlie, what do you want from me?" he finally wailed, leaning against the wall.

Charlie grinned. "What does any decent blackmailer want? Money, of course. Now, if you were to find . . . say . . . twenty-five bucks for me, I could take off after my lesson and buy some new CDs. You know, I've really been wanting to build up my polka collection!"

Winston frowned and decided to ignore that polka-collection comment. "I don't have that much money on me."

"Well, when will you get it?" Charlie demanded.

Good question, Winston thought. He didn't know when he was going to have any money in the foreseeable future. *How about when I sell my accordion at the pawn shop?* "As—as soon as possible?" Winston said, smiling at Charlie.

Charlie nodded. "Right answer. You've got a week—until Monday. I'll be in touch, Egghead." He went back into Mr. Pagnowski's office, closing the door behind him.

Winston exhaled and slumped against the wall. Twenty-five dollars by next Monday? He didn't even have twenty-five *cents!*

"So, are you ready for our first encounter with the Riccoli kids?" Elizabeth asked Jessica as they pedaled up the hill toward Mrs. Riccoli's house on Monday just before six o'clock.

"I'm ready. And if we keep working here, I'm going to get in terrific shape." Jessica panted as they headed up the driveway on their bicycles.

Elizabeth smiled. "I think the kids are going to give us the best workout of all." She didn't know exactly how she and Jessica would handle five of them at once, but she figured they could rely on each other. And Mrs. Riccoli pointed out that her oldest daughter, Olivia, could help the twins take care of the younger kids. Olivia was ten, only a couple of years younger than the twins themselves.

Elizabeth got off her bicycle and leaned it against a hedge by the side of the house, next to Jessica's.

"This is weird," Jessica commented.

"What? Baby-sitting?" Elizabeth asked, putting her knapsack over her shoulder.

"No. There aren't any lights on," Jessica observed.

Elizabeth glanced up at the house as they walked up the porch stairs. Jessica was right—the house looked completely dark. Dusk was setting, and because it had been such a cloudy day and the house was surrounded by large trees, the whole scene was very dark. "Why wouldn't they have the lights on?" Elizabeth wondered out loud.

"Maybe they're taking naps or something," Jessica said with a shrug, pressing the doorbell.

"Or maybe their electricity isn't hooked up yet?" Elizabeth suggested.

"*Please*. Like anyone could live without it," Jessica said.

"Some people do," Elizabeth argued.

Jessica rolled her eyes. "Yeah. Abraham Lincoln." She pressed the doorbell again. "I don't think this thing's working."

Elizabeth knocked on the wood door a couple of times. Then she banged on it again, as hard as she could.

"Don't break it down!" Jessica said.

"As if I could." Elizabeth frowned. "Don't you think this is kind of strange? Where are they? Maybe they had to go out for something." She paced back and forth on the porch, looking around the expansive yard.

"No, I think they're home. There's the car." Jessica pointed to a blue minivan in the driveway.

"They could have walked somewhere," Elizabeth observed.

"With five kids? I doubt it." Jessica tried peering in one of the windows. "Are you *sure* Mrs. Riccoli said six o'clock?"

"Of course I'm sure," Elizabeth replied, chewing her thumbnail. "I was there, remember?"

"Well, excuse me!" Jessica said.

"Look, let's not argue. It's a huge house. They could be upstairs and just not hear us. I think we should go in," Elizabeth said. "What do you think?"

Jessica shrugged. "Sure, I guess so."

Elizabeth had a feeling that she and Jessica were

only fighting because they were both nervous. Even though she knew it was ridiculous, Elizabeth couldn't help feeling a little intimidated by the creaky old house as Jessica slowly opened the front door. She'd never been inside, and she'd heard so many rumors about it. The winding stairs someone had once fallen down. Giant spiders hiding in the spooky, cobweb-filled basement, waiting to crawl on your neck. The ghost that haunted the third floor.

"Jessica?" she said softly. "Do you really think this place is still . . . haunted?"

"No way," Jessica declared boldly. But her voice shook as she quietly called, "H-hel-hello?" into the dark, cavernous front hallway.

Nobody answered. Upstairs a floorboard creaked, as if somebody had taken a step.

"M-maybe we should get out of here," Jessica said, shooting Elizabeth a panicked look.

Elizabeth nodded quickly. "Let's go. We can wait outside."

"Good idea." Jessica turned around and Elizabeth followed her, tiptoeing quietly toward the door.

Suddenly a loud, horrifying scream pierced the air. At the same time lights started flashing on and off in all the downstairs rooms. An evil, loud, creepy cackle floated down the stairs.

"*Aaaahhhhh!*" Jessica and Elizabeth screamed, and ran straight out the door.

Three

Jessica and Elizabeth didn't stop running until they reached the driveway. Jessica put her hand to her throat, trying to catch her breath. Her heart felt like it was beating a million times a minute. "I am . . . never . . . going in that . . . house . . . again," she managed to gasp.

"N-neither am I," Elizabeth stammered, her face flushed pink. "Forget about earning money!"

"Forget about my new miniskirt! Nothing's worth—" Jessica stopped. She thought she heard something else coming from the house—another kind of noise altogether. "Did you hear that?"

"What?" Elizabeth looked even more panicked.

"Listen," Jessica urged, taking a few steps back up the sidewalk.

"What are you doing?" Elizabeth asked. "Are you

crazy?" She reached out to grab Jessica's arm.

"No," Jessica said, her eyes flashing as she stared at the front door of the house. She wasn't crazy. Unless you counted the fact that she was crazy enough to actually baby-sit for a bunch of practical jokers! "Elizabeth, look!" She pointed to the house, where the Riccoli kids were all on the porch, laughing and giggling.

"You mean they . . ." Elizabeth shook her head. "They did that? They got us?"

"They *totally* got us," Jessica admitted, frowning at the kids, who were still doubled over with laughter. She didn't see what was so funny about scaring her half to death! If this was what working for the Riccolis was going to be like, maybe she should forget about her new outfit and wear last year's clothes instead.

She looked down at her worn-out pair of Doc Martens. OK, so maybe that was being a *bit* drastic.

"Kids! What are you up now?" Mrs. Riccoli shouted from an upstairs bedroom window.

All five kids immediately stopped laughing. A few of them scampered out onto the yard and pretended to be innocently playing.

"Nothing, Mom!" Andrew called up to her. "Look, our baby-sitters are here!"

"Oh, no. Hello, girls!" Mrs. Riccoli waved. "Sorry about that. They like to welcome all their new baby-sitters with a little practical joke. I guess they thought scaring you would be fun."

"Oh, it was a lot of fun," Jessica muttered under her breath.

"I'll be right down!" Mrs. Riccoli called to them, disappearing back inside.

"Do you think they know that their house is supposed to be haunted?" Elizabeth asked as they walked back toward the porch. "Or was their deciding to scare us just a rotten coincidence?"

"They had to know," Jessica grumbled. "They couldn't be that lucky."

Andrew ran over to the twins. "You should have seen your faces! You guys freaked out!" he told them happily.

"Well, you would, too, if somebody did that to you," Elizabeth said.

"Not that we would, because we're a lot more *considerate*," Jessica added. "You'd better not do that again."

Andrew looked up at her, his lips pursed in a huge pout. Jessica felt an unexpected pang of her least favorite emotion—guilt. She had to admit that they were cute kids, even if they were major troublemakers. "At least—don't do it again tonight, OK? Because if you do, then Elizabeth and I will have to scare you back," she said mischievously.

"You will?" Andrew seemed very excited at the prospect.

Jessica nodded. "Uh-huh. Only we'll wait for a really good time. Like when you're completely unprepared!" She reached out to tickle him.

Andrew squealed. "I won't be scared of *you*."

"We'll see," Jessica said, tickling his neck.

"Noooo!" he cried, running away.

Elizabeth laughed. "I think this is going to be a great job, actually. You know, you're kind of good with kids."

"Don't sound so surprised! It's not like I haven't done this before." Jessica looked at the kids, who were all playing a game of leapfrog on the lawn. Nate was struggling to hop over Olivia, and she stood up and started carrying him piggyback around the yard. They *were* awfully cute. OK, so they had an obnoxious streak, but it was nothing she couldn't handle. "So they scared us a little," she said to Elizabeth. "It's not like the house is *really* haunted. I mean, how could any house stay haunted with those guys around, right?"

"Right," Elizabeth agreed with a nervous smile. "Let's go in and say hi to Mrs. Riccoli." She started up the sidewalk.

Jessica knew she shouldn't be afraid. Still, her legs felt a little shaky as they climbed the stairs to the porch. What *about* all those old rumors of the mansion? Weren't rumors based on the truth . . . at least some of the time? Even the rumors at school usually had a hint of truth in them. *And if just a little bit of what I heard about this place is true . . .*

Jessica stepped gingerly across the porch beside Elizabeth and into the house, which was now all lit up. Jessica's eyes widened. She'd never seen such ugly furniture in her entire life! The Riccolis had one of the most beautiful houses in town, on the outside. But inside—that was another story!

In the living room there was an orange shag rug, a red plaid couch, and red-and-pink-striped beanbag chairs. Jessica shuddered. It was like looking at someone with a really, really bad outfit on. And the Riccolis actually lived with that every day! In fact, if Jessica was going to spend her nights baby-sitting and hanging out there, *she* would have to look at it, too.

Or would she? Jessica's mind whirled. Her mother was an interior designer—maybe she'd have a few helpful decorating ideas. Like replacing all the furniture, rugs, and curtains. Jessica didn't want to offend Mrs. Riccoli. But she was going to have to tell her that whoever decorated her living room needed a new pair of prescription glasses.

This is going to work out perfectly! she thought, excited. Jessica knew that her mother had been looking for new clients ever since she had bought a new minivan for the family—and if her mother had more money, then it only naturally followed that *Jessica* would get some of it. . . .

That's all there is to it. Mom's going to have to do an emergency makeover on this place, Jessica thought as she and Elizabeth waited for Mrs. Riccoli to come downstairs. *Immediately if not sooner!* Jessica stared at a brown tree-shaped lamp with a green, leaf-decorated shade. *Talk about scary!* she thought as Mrs. Riccoli came down the stairs.

*   *   *

"I win! I win!" Gretchen cried, throwing her arms into the air. She jumped off the floor and started dancing around the room. "I'm the Chutes and Ladders champion of all time!"

"It's a stupid game, anyway," Andrew complained.

"Beaten by a seven-year-old," Elizabeth said, shaking her head as she looked down at the game board. "I can't believe it. I must be getting too old." She smiled at Juliana, who was sitting beside her.

"You're, like, really old," the five-year-old replied, rolling her eyes.

Elizabeth reached over and ruffled Juliana's long, curly brown hair. "I am?"

"You're like—a dinosaur!" Andrew added. "Elizabeth is a stegosaurus and Jessica is a—"

"Brontosaurus!" Gretchen chimed in.

Andrew started reassembling all the game pieces at the starting line. "Let's play again!"

"Well, I don't know," Jessica said, glancing at the large square red clock on the wall. "It's getting kind of late. Your mom said you guys go to bed at eight."

"No, we don't!" Gretchen cried.

"Yeah!" Juliana added. "We can stay up until ten!"

"Really?" Elizabeth asked, raising her eyebrows. "You don't say." She knew getting so many kids to bed at once was going to be a problem.

"No, you guys have to be in bed by the time Mom gets home," Olivia, the oldest, said. "Because if you aren't, *I'm* going to be in big trouble."

"Olivia has a point," Elizabeth said, nodding. "You wouldn't want to get her in trouble, would you?" *Actually, yes, they probably would!* she thought, remembering how she and Jessica had tortured their older brother, Steven, when he used to baby-sit for them.

"Well, maybe Gretchen and Juliana should go to bed, but *I* can stay up because I'm older!" Andrew declared. "I want some more of those brownies."

"We ate them all," Jessica told him with a shrug. "So you see, there's not even any good reason to stay up, is there?"

"TV!" Andrew, Gretchen, and Juliana yelled.

"Sorry. No can do," Elizabeth said. She was starting to feel incredibly lucky that Nate, the two-year-old, had gone to sleep without a hitch at seven. He was apparently worn out from chasing Elizabeth all over the house for a good half hour. "So, who's coming upstairs?" She stood up and smiled at the circle of kids sitting on the floor.

"I am!" Jessica said, jumping to her feet.

Gretchen giggled. "You're not going to sleep, silly!"

"That's what you think," Jessica said. "Whoever gets upstairs last doesn't get a bed!" She raced for the stairs and Andrew and Gretchen followed her, running at top speed and pushing each other out of the way.

"I'm going to do some homework in my room," Olivia told Elizabeth, standing up.

"OK. I'll come check on you later." Elizabeth smiled as Olivia climbed the stairs. Then she turned to Juliana. "Aren't you afraid Jessica's going to take your bed? You'd better hurry!"

Juliana shrugged. "I don't care. I don't want to go to bed."

"I know. But you have to eventually," Elizabeth said. "You don't want to be tired tomorrow morning at kindergarten."

Juliana played with the game pieces, pushing them up and down the chutes and ladders. She didn't look like she was going anywhere. Elizabeth wondered if she was like this every night.

"How about if I go upstairs with you? Would that help?" Elizabeth asked, hoping she just wanted some company. Elizabeth remembered how lonely she used to feel when she had a new baby-sitter who she didn't know that well.

Juliana nodded shyly. Elizabeth took her hand and helped pull her up, and together they walked up the long, circular stairs to the second floor. She wondered why Juliana seemed so sad. Then it hit her—maybe it was because her father hadn't moved with them. Maybe he was the one who usually put her to bed! "I bet you miss your dad," Elizabeth said to Juliana. "Do you?"

"Yes!" Juliana said. She went into her room and pulled a pair of sleeveless pink pajamas out from underneath her pillow. "I wish he would hurry up and get here!"

"I know how that feels. And you know what? I bet he misses you just as much as you miss him,"

Elizabeth said, looking at all the posters of horses and dolls on the walls while Juliana changed. "He's probably sitting at your old house right now, feeling sad about it."

"He called us before you guys came over!" Juliana said, sounding a little more cheerful as she slid underneath the covers. "He said he's going to call us every single day at least twice until he moves."

Elizabeth perched on the edge of the bed. "That sounds like a good idea. So, do you want me to read you a story? Would that help you fall asleep?"

Juliana shook her head. "I don't want to fall asleep."

Elizabeth gave her a concerned look. Most kids didn't want to go to bed—but once they got into bed, they usually didn't mind falling asleep. Maybe Juliana was afraid of the dark or something. "How come you don't want to fall asleep?" she asked Juliana.

"I don't like to sleep." Juliana's mouth turned downward in a frown. "I have bad dreams."

Elizabeth put her hand on Juliana's arm. "We all have bad dreams sometimes. That's OK! I know I do. And I hate them, too." She made a funny face and stuck out her tongue. "They're horrible! But I'm sure you don't have bad dreams every night."

"Yes, I do," Juliana protested. "Ever since we moved here!"

"Really?" Elizabeth pondered Juliana's face. She looked frightened. "Well, maybe it's because you moved to this big new house. You've only been here a couple of days. I bet it doesn't feel like home yet."

"No. That's not it," Juliana said. "I like it here! But in my dreams there's this monster girl and she's trying to hurt me!"

A monster girl? Elizabeth thought. *That doesn't sound good.* She wondered if maybe Juliana had been bullied by someone at her new kindergarten. "And you've had the same bad dream more than once?" Elizabeth asked, concerned.

Juliana nodded, clutching the covers tightly around her neck. "Ever since we got here."

Elizabeth watched as Juliana covered her face with the comforter. She couldn't help feeling that something kind of strange was going on. Juliana was very afraid—but of a dream? Why? "Well, you know what?" she said gently. "Sometimes when something else is bothering us, we have these bad dreams. But now you've been here a couple of days, so you're more used to it. And you like your new kindergarten teacher, and you've made some friends at school, right? I bet there's no way you could have a bad dream tonight!"

"Really?" Juliana asked, sounding hopeful as she pulled the comforter off her face. Her brown eyes looked sleepy when she smiled.

"Sure," Elizabeth said. "Just think about all the fun things you're going to do in Sweet Valley. We have this really great zoo. And there's a huge video arcade at the mall. And then there's the beach—maybe we can go there next weekend."

"Mm," Juliana mumbled.

"Nothing in your dreams can hurt you," Elizabeth said softly. "Don't worry. I'll be right here."

A few minutes later Juliana drifted off to sleep. Elizabeth turned off the light on her night table and sat for a few minutes, watching the little girl sleep. She couldn't imagine why Juliana was having such scary dreams. Something had to really be bothering her.

It must just be the move, Elizabeth decided, tucking the end of the sheet under the mattress. Moving was hard on anybody, but especially a young child. *I'll have to keep an eye on her and make sure she's handling it OK.*

"So, you two are still alive—that's a good sign," Mrs. Riccoli joked, setting her brown leather brief-case on the kitchen table.

"It was great," Jessica said, wiping her hands on a plaid dish towel. After putting the kids to bed, she and Elizabeth had quickly cleaned up the mess the kids had made when they had "helped" the twins bake brownies.

This baby-sitting thing was much easier than Jessica had thought. After she got over the kids' practical joke, she'd actually started to enjoy herself. Already Gretchen was saying she wanted to be just like Jessica when she grew up. *Of course, I'm not surprised. I knew one of them would idolize me eventually.* "Everything went fine," she told Mrs. Riccoli. "Didn't it, Elizabeth?"

"No problems," Elizabeth said, sliding the clean brownie pan back into the cabinet. "Except . . . I had a hard time getting Juliana to go to sleep. She told me she's been having nightmares lately. Did you know about that?"

"Yes, unfortunately. She hasn't been sleeping through the night much," Mrs. Riccoli said, slipping off her navy blazer. "But I'm sure it'll pass. Kids have bad dreams more than you'd think—especially when there's something big going on."

"Like a big move?" Jessica asked.

"Exactly. Don't worry about it, Elizabeth. But thanks for mentioning it to me. And thanks so much for helping me out tonight." Mrs. Riccoli opened her wallet and handed a ten-dollar bill to Jessica and one to Elizabeth.

Jessica grinned. "You're welcome!" At this rate she was going to be rich in no time. Two more nights and she could get that new pair of brown jeans she wanted. "When do you need us again?" she asked eagerly.

"Not until Wednesday," Mrs. Riccoli said. "Same time?"

Jessica groaned. "I can't. I have a Unicorn Club meeting."

"I'll ask Amy," Elizabeth offered. "Maybe she can help me."

Jessica frowned. She briefly considered skipping her meeting, but she knew Lila and everyone else would never forgive her. So now Amy was going to get *her money*. And Jessica really did deserve the money—after all, if she hadn't insisted that she and Elizabeth take a look at the moving truck on Saturday, they wouldn't even know about the Riccolis' gold mine of baby-sitting in the first place. Life wasn't fair.

"Can you girls get home OK on your bikes?" Mrs. Riccoli asked. "Or do you want a ride?"

"It's OK—we have bike lights, and we don't live too far from here," Elizabeth said.

"All right, then. See you Wednesday, I guess. Thanks again." Mrs. Riccoli smiled.

Jessica went into the living room to grab her jacket and tiny blue knapsack. They were lying on one of the striped pink-and-red beanbag chairs. Staring at the horrid shag rug, she remembered— she had to talk to Mrs. Riccoli!

"Just a second," she told Elizabeth as Mrs. Riccoli walked into the room. "Mrs. Riccoli? You know, the hardwood floors under this rug are really, really beautiful. I mean, they could be, if you refinished them. And if you did, you wouldn't need this rug." Jessica stepped around the beanbag chairs. "Then you could get like an oak futon, with a cover that matches . . . and some nice matching curtains." She swept her arm through the air, indicating the areas she was talking about. "And maybe you could also pick up some antique furniture that kind of goes along with the style of the house? You know, the period thing, or whatever they call it. Victorian. Because Victorian and beanbags . . . well, you kind of don't think of those things in the same sentence, you know?"

She glanced over at Elizabeth, who was loudly clearing her throat. Elizabeth stared back at her, looking completely horrified. "Jessica, what are you talking about?"

But Mrs. Riccoli smiled. "I get the distinct feeling that you don't like what I've done with this room. Or should I say, what I haven't done?"

Jessica blushed. "I'm sorry. I don't mean to be so critical." *It just happens. Like, when I see something I can't stand.* "It's just that my mom is an interior designer, and she's redone a lot of the old houses in the area. And I thought—maybe, you know. She could take a look, give you some ideas?"

"Jessica," Elizabeth said sternly, "if Mrs. Riccoli wants help, she can ask, but you don't—"

Mrs. Riccoli held out her hand. "Help. I'm asking. Do you have one of your mother's business cards?"

"Sure!" Jessica said. "Let me find it—I carry one in my wallet." She rummaged in her knapsack until she found her wallet, then plucked out the dog-eared card and handed it to Mrs. Riccoli. "She's really, really good. And she's an expert at renovating old houses."

"Well, if her ideas are anything like yours, I'll be interested," Mrs. Riccoli said, nodding. She looked at the rug and sighed. "I guess this rug has seen better days. It's just that with the kids being such a handful the past several years, and Fred and I working full-time, we really haven't been able to pay any attention to stuff like this."

"Oh, I understand," Elizabeth said. "I mean, you're really busy."

"Busy is an understatement." Mrs. Riccoli laughed. "More like completely crazed."

"So that's where our mom comes in," Jessica said. "She won't do anything unless you like it, and she won't make it expensive, either." Jessica's mother was going to be so thrilled when Jessica got home and sprang the news on her about getting her a new client!

She hoped she hadn't offended Mrs. Riccoli, but she struck Jessica as the kind of person who appreciated the truth. And if there was one true thing about this house, it was that the place needed to be fixed up.

"Well, thanks for the referral," Mrs. Riccoli said. "I'll call her later in the week. I *would* like to get rid of these beanbag chairs—they were my husband's in college, and he just can't seem to part with them. But since he's still in Sacramento . . ." She rubbed her palms together. "This is the perfect opportunity to get rid of them!"

Elizabeth laughed. "What will you say when he asks what happened to them?"

"Simple. The movers lost them." Mrs. Riccoli grinned. "I think, actually, they're going to lose a *lot* of things. Tell your mother I'll be in touch soon."

"Great! Thanks again," Jessica said as she and Elizabeth went out the front door.

Elizabeth nudged her sister once they were alone.

"Jessica, did you have to insult her? You weren't exactly tactful, you know."

"Elizabeth, there's no tactful way to say that someone's house needs a major overhaul." Jessica walked down the steps and turned to walk around the corner, where their bikes were. "It's like on those talk shows when they do ambush makeovers on people's best friends because they really, really need it or deserve it or whatever. I mean, you just have to plunge in and be honest because if you're not, then you're not doing that person any favors and—"

A tall figure suddenly stepped in front of her, blocking the light from the porch.

"Eeek!" Jessica squealed, stepping backward. She crashed right into Elizabeth, whose sneakers slipped on the wet grass, making a loud squeak.

"Whoa!" Elizabeth cried, grabbing the branch of a hedge to catch her balance. "Who—who are you?"

Four

◇

The tall figure stepped forward, and in the dim light Jessica could vaguely make out an older man, wearing overalls and a T-shirt. He had gray hair, and Jessica noticed that he was carrying a hose with one hand and a pair of large clippers in the other.

"I'm sorry. I didn't mean to bump into you," the man said in a gravelly voice.

"Ahem! Likewise." Jessica brushed a hedge branch away from where it was poking into her sleeve. The nerve of some people! What was this guy up to, anyway, creeping around outside the Riccolis' with a pair of clippers in his hand? Didn't he know this was private property? "What are you doing out here?" she demanded, suddenly feeling protective on Mrs. Riccoli's behalf.

"I am Mr. Brangwen. I am the gardener here," he announced.

"The gardener?" Jessica repeated. "Oh." So that explained the clippers. Kind of.

"Well, you're working kind of late, aren't you?" Elizabeth asked, sounding suspicious.

"Yeah!" Jessica added. "How can you even see what you're doing?" For some reason she didn't trust this guy.

"As any half-decent gardener knows, this is the best time to do the watering and clipping," he replied coldly. "And who exactly are you?"

"I'm Jessica, and this is Elizabeth. We're the new baby-sitters," Jessica said. *And we're going to be watching you!* "And now if it's OK with you, we need to get our bikes and go home before our parents have a fit."

Mr. Brangwen glared at her. "So you're the ones who left your bikes leaning against the hedges?"

Jessica took a step away from him. His eyes were so intense—as if he hated her or something! "Yeah," she said slowly. "Those are our bikes."

"You should not do that," Mr. Brangwen said sternly. "You could damage the branches. Next time you come, leave them in the garage. The hedges need air and light to be healthy. Promise me you will never do that again!"

"You really care about this place, don't you?" Elizabeth observed.

In a nutty kind of way, Jessica felt like adding.

"I ought to. I have been the gardener here

for my entire life," Mr. Brangwen said.

"Really? Even when it was all deserted and haunted and weird?" Jessica asked.

Mr. Brangwen stared at her, his eyes still intense. Jessica felt a little tremor in her hand as she ran it through her hair, trying to act casual. There was something very creepy about him, Jessica decided. Or else he really didn't like her at all. Which was creepy enough on its own.

"Not that it is any of your business, but I am devoted to this house. And I will continue to work here until all my work is done!" Mr. Brangwen declared fiercely.

Jessica laughed nervously. "Yeah, well. A job's a job, I guess." She tugged at Elizabeth's sleeve. "We'd better go."

Elizabeth was staring up at Mr. Brangwen with a perplexed expression on her face. "You worked here that whole time?"

"Yes. And I want to warn you both. You two should be very careful around here," Mr. Brangwen said ominously.

"We won't leave our bikes against the hedge next time, I promise," Jessica said quickly. Boy, talk about being obsessed with your work! She was starting to change her mind about Mr. Brangwen. He wasn't scary. He was crazy!

"Not that. I must warn you about the house," he said quietly, almost in a whisper. "Never close your eyes in that house. Never!"

"Yeah, OK," Jessica said. "Whatever you say.

Come *on*, Elizabeth." She pulled her sister over to their bikes. They quickly got on, turned on their bikes' front headlights and rear flashing red lights, and headed down the driveway.

"What he said just then—wasn't that weird?" Elizabeth asked once they were out of earshot.

"The guy's weird, so everything he says is going to be weird," Jessica declared. "Don't tell me you believed him."

"Well, I wouldn't, normally. But tonight, when I was putting Juliana to bed, she was afraid to fall asleep. And he just told us not to close our eyes," Elizabeth mused, shifting gears. "Do you think maybe those two things are connected?"

"First of all, Elizabeth." Jessica stopped at a stop sign and waited for a few cars to pass. "How could we possibly close our eyes when we're at Mrs. Riccoli's? We have five kids to look after! And second of all, I think Mr. Brangwen is just a grumpy old gardener who has nothing better to do than sit around acting like the hedge police."

Elizabeth giggled. "He *was* kind of overly upset with us about the silly hedges."

"Next time I go there I'm leaving my bike in the flower bed just to bug him!" Jessica declared, pushing off from the curb.

"Winston! Could you get that?" Mrs. Egbert called from the kitchen Monday night. "My hands are full with this pot roast!"

Winston picked up the cordless phone from the coffee table in the living room. He had been leafing through his science textbook on the couch, practically dozing off. As he pressed the on button to answer the phone, he had a chilling thought. What if it was Charlie, demanding his money?

Be a man about it, Winston told himself, trying to summon his courage. *A very scared man, but still.* "Hello?" he said brightly.

"Hello. Is this the number for the Five Friends Baby-sitting Service?" a woman asked.

Winston cleared his throat and sat up straighter. "Yes, it is," he said. He couldn't believe it—Elizabeth had told him she was going to post a few signs at the Savvy Shopper Supermarket, but she hadn't mentioned putting *his* phone number on the signs. "How can we help you?" Winston asked, trying to sound professional.

"Well, I desperately need a baby-sitter for Thursday night," the woman said. "Oh! I'm sorry, I should have introduced myself. My name is Mrs. Karsten. And my husband and I need to go to a business function this Thursday from about six to nine. Could you take care of our twins?"

"Twins?" Winston repeated.

"Yes. They're eight months old, and they're not much trouble. We'll have everything all set up for you, too," Mrs. Karsten said.

"Oh, sure," Winston said, his mind whirling. The sooner he took a baby-sitting job, the sooner he'd be able to pay Charlie. "That would be no problem!" Besides, twins—that almost sounded fun. After all, Jessica and Elizabeth were twins, and *they* were a lot of fun. He had a lot of experience dealing with twins who had completely different personalities. Did eight-month-old babies have personalities? Winston wasn't sure. "I would definitely be able to help you out. That's this Thursday at six. What's your address?" he asked Mrs. Karsten.

"Well, wait a second. Let me ask you a couple of questions first. Have you done much baby-sitting?" Mrs. Karsten asked.

"Oh . . . we've been in business for years," Winston said. "Not officially, of course. But I've done a lot of baby-sitting. In fact, last summer I took care of my little cousins almost every day." Never mind that his cousins were nine and ten, two years younger than Winston. He'd still made them peanut butter sandwiches, hadn't he?

"And do you have experience taking care of infants?" Mrs. Karsten wanted to know. "Karla and Kevin are still very young—"

"Karla and Kevin Karsten? Oh, I love it," Winston gushed. *Even if it is a little too . . . kute.* "Mrs. Karsten, babies are like . . . my life." *At least, until I pay off Charlie, they will be,* Winston thought. He couldn't let anyone at school find out about his new hobby, the accordion, or his social life would be over. It was hard enough to get any respect at school—if anyone found out about that dumb, unfortunate instrument that looked like a piano with fins, he was sunk.

"Good! Then I'll see you Thursday. Come by at around a quarter to six so I can show you everything, all right? Wait—let me give you my phone number and address," Mrs. Karsten said.

Winston grabbed a pen off the coffee table and jotted down the information, grinning. He was booked for Thursday. If he could get one more baby-sitting job that week, he'd have enough money for Charlie—and maybe some left over!

Jessica came downstairs on Tuesday morning for breakfast, rubbing her eyes. She'd had to do some of her homework after she got home from the Riccolis' house, so she'd stayed up later than usual, and she was still feeling tired. *Tired . . . but rich,* she thought, remembering the ten-dollar bill she had stashed in her sock drawer. She'd earn a ton of money baby-sitting for Mrs. Riccoli. Then, if she got a raise in her allowance by bringing her grades up, there would be no stopping her the next time she hit the mall!

"How was the baby-sitting job last night?" Mrs. Wakefield asked as Jessica set her backpack on the stairs. "I didn't get a chance to ask you when you got home. You practically flew upstairs to start your homework."

"Hurrying to start homework?" Mr. Wakefield asked. "That sounds impressive."

Jessica smiled at him. *With the right motivation, anything's possible.* She slid into the chair next to her mother and sleepily picked up the glass of orange juice that had already been poured for her. "I got all my homework done. And the baby-sitting was great!"

"Oh, yeah," said her older brother, Steven, rolling his eyes. "I bet it was thrilling."

"I had fun," Elizabeth insisted. "We both did. The kids are cute and pretty well behaved, considering they're so young. I think it'll be nice working there."

Jessica set her empty glass on the table and reached for the plate of toast. "Except for this totally bizarre gardener who practically accosted us when we tried to get our bikes."

"Accosted you?" Jessica's father looked alarmed. "What do you mean?"

"It wasn't like that, Dad," Elizabeth said. "I mean, he did seem kind of strange, but—"

"Kind of?" Jessica interjected.

Elizabeth giggled. "He got mad at us because we left our bikes leaning against the hedges."

"Yeah, and he thought we were going to kill all the plants on the property," Jessica said. "Then he started saying something weird about—what was it? I can't even remember. Anyway, that's not the biggest news. Mom, I think I got you a job!"

"As their new gardener?" Mrs. Wakefield joked.

"No, as their new decorator," Jessica said. She crunched into a piece of wheat toast spread with thick strawberry jam. "And man, do they need one."

"Jessica," Mr. Wakefield said. "That's not a very nice thing to say."

"Yeah. Have you looked at your *room* lately?" Steven teased. "If anyone needs a decorator—"

"The point is, Mom," Jessica interrupted, dismissing her brother with a wave of her hand, "Mrs. Riccoli needs to have some work done, so I gave her your card, and she said she'd call you. Isn't that great? I mean, you said business was kind of slow lately, and I know you were worried about spending all that money on the new minivan. Now your problems are solved!"

Mrs. Wakefield smiled. "Of course, I can always use new clients. Is it a big job?"

"The hugest," Jessica said. "Do the words *orange shag* mean anything to you?"

"Jessica . . . ," her father said in a warning tone.

"Besides," Jessica went on. "It's a really big house, with tons of rooms. Isn't it, Elizabeth?"

"It's very big," Elizabeth agreed. "But we can't sit around talking interior decorating anymore or we're going to be late for school."

"Oh, what a shame, you're leaving?" Steven asked sarcastically. "But the conversation's going to be so dull."

"Like you, you mean?" Jessica replied.

Elizabeth stood up and grabbed her backpack from beside the door. "Come on, Jessica. We'd better go."

"Which house is the Riccolis', exactly?" Mrs. Wakefield asked as Jessica got her backpack from the stairs.

"I'll tell you all about it later!" Jessica promised her mother, opening the door to leave. Getting a detention for being late wouldn't exactly help her grade-point average. "I have some fantastic ideas for what to do with the living room!"

Elizabeth stared at the Riccolis' television, her heart pounding in her throat.

The monster was creeping around the corner of the house. The night sky was completely dark, except for a small sliver of moonlight that glinted off the knife the monster was carrying behind his back. Inside the house a man was lying in bed, reading a book, completely unaware that the monster was about to break into his house.

"I can't watch," Elizabeth whispered to Amy, who was sitting on the couch beside her. "It's too scary!"

Amy was staring at the television, her face completely pale.

It was Wednesday night, and Elizabeth and Amy had sat down to watch *Monster Mania III* after finally getting all the Riccoli kids to settle down and fall asleep.

"Oh, no," Elizabeth said, watching the monster slowly turn the handle on the back door. "He's going into the house!"

Amy sucked in her breath. Her eyes were focused so intently on the screen, she looked like she was in a trance.

Elizabeth chewed her thumbnail, cringing as the movie soundtrack plunged into plaintive piano music. She watched as the monster slipped into the house and made his way upstairs to where the man was reading. With each step the creepy music got louder and louder, becoming even scarier and more off-key. Elizabeth gripped the arm of the couch tightly as the monster pushed open the door.

"No! No! No!"

A loud shriek rang out upstairs and Elizabeth jumped to her feet, her heart pounding. "What— what—was th-that?"

"I don't know!" Amy said, clutching the wool afghan blanket on her lap.

"No! Stay away!" the voice screeched.

"It's one of the kids!" Amy said, getting up quickly. "I thought it was in the movie or—"

"That's Juliana!" Elizabeth realized. "She's having a nightmare!" She and Amy dashed into the hallway and flew up the stairs, heading straight for Juliana's bedroom. Elizabeth ran in and flipped on the overhead light.

Juliana was thrashing from side to side in her bed, the sheets and blanket a twisted tangle around her. "No! No, you can't!" she yelled.

Elizabeth ran to Juliana's side and touched her shoulder, shaking her gently. "Juliana, wake up. Wake up, it's OK!"

Juliana blinked a few times and looked at Elizabeth. "Elizabeth!" she cried. "It was—it was *her*!" She burst into tears.

"Her?" Elizabeth suddenly remembered Juliana telling her about the monster girl who was trying to "get" her. Apparently the same girl was still frightening Juliana in her dreams. *But why?* Elizabeth wondered.

Elizabeth reached out and gathered Juliana in a tight hug. "It's all right. She can't hurt you now." She released Juliana, brushing the tears off her cheeks with her fingers. "Don't cry. Amy and I are here, and we're going to make sure nobody hurts you."

"Elizabeth's right." Amy handed Juliana a tissue.

"But—that girl. She was trying to *kill* me!" Juliana protested.

Trying to kill her? This sounds like a serious nightmare, Elizabeth thought. She wondered if she should mention it to Mrs. Riccoli. *No*, she decided. *She already has too much to deal with, and she knows more about her kids' nightmares than I do!*

"What's going on?" Andrew was standing in the doorway, blinking in the bright light.

"Juliana had a nightmare, but she's OK now," Elizabeth told him quickly. She didn't want Andrew to get scared, too. "Everything's fine. You can go back to bed."

"Hey, I'll come with you," Amy offered. She disappeared down the hall, ushering Andrew back to his room.

"Do you feel any better now?" Elizabeth asked, looking down at Juliana, who was sitting up in bed, hugging her pillow. "You know that girl can't hurt you, don't you?"

Juliana nodded. "I guess. But it sure *feels* like she's going to."

"This girl you dream about . . . it's not somebody you know, is it? Someone at school, maybe, who isn't very nice to you?" Elizabeth asked.

Juliana shook her head vehemently.

"Oh." *So much for that theory!* "Well, if she isn't real, then she definitely can't get you!" she reasoned.

"I don't care," Juliana said. "She's icky. And I'm not going back to sleep. I'm never sleeping again!"

"You can't do *that*, silly," Elizabeth said. "Imagine how tired you'd get! This would be you, walking to school tomorrow." She stood up and walked around Juliana's room, imitating a sleepwalker. "You wouldn't be Juliana anymore—you'd be a zombie!"

Juliana giggled a little. Then she frowned. "I don't care. I'm still not sleeping. I'll have that same dream, I know I will!"

To Elizabeth's relief, Amy came back into the room at that moment. Elizabeth was running out of comforting things to say to Juliana.

Fortunately Amy came to her rescue. "You know, Juliana, I used to have this recurring nightmare, too. Recurring means that you have the same dream over and over," she explained, sitting down on the edge of Juliana's bed. "I hated it!"

"What was it about?" Juliana asked, her eyes wide with fear.

"Well, I kept having this dream that tigers were chasing me through this dark, dense forest—and I'd always wake up just when they were about to catch me! I'd scream and scream until my mom came into the room."

"So how did you get it to stop?" Elizabeth asked.

Amy shrugged. "They just . . . stopped. That's all. I woke up one morning and I realized that I wasn't having them anymore, and I was so happy—just like you're going to be when you quit having your bad dream," she told Juliana confidently.

"Yeah, but . . . my dreams are real," Juliana insisted. "That girl was going to hurt me!"

"I thought the tigers were going to get me, too. But they didn't," Amy said. "See, I'm here, and I'm fine."

"You know what? There's this dream I have over and over, too," Elizabeth suddenly remembered.

"The one where you meet Johnny Buck and he asks you to marry him?" Amy teased.

Juliana giggled.

"No." Elizabeth shook her head, relieved to see a smile on the little girl's face. And she had a feeling her smile was about to get a *lot* bigger. "It's . . . well, this is pretty embarrassing." Elizabeth could feel her face turning bright pink. "I'm at school in this dream, and I'm going to this assembly, and I have to give a big speech. So I get up on the stage, and I'm about to start talking when I look down and realize—I don't have any clothes on!"

Both Amy and Juliana burst out laughing.

Elizabeth shrugged. "Pretty silly, huh?"

"Just as long as it never happens," Amy said.

"It won't! See, that's what I'm trying to tell you, Juliana. Your dreams can never *happen* in real life. At least . . . I hope not." Elizabeth laughed.

"You would be in big trouble if they did," Juliana said, poking Elizabeth's leg.

"I think that would be a speech no one would *ever* forget!" Amy added, and the three of them broke into hysterical giggles again.

"All right, OK, will everyone just get *over* it already?" Elizabeth asked through her giggles. She *was* a little embarrassed, but she was glad to have cheered up Juliana. Juliana didn't even seem to be thinking about the girl in her nightmare anymore.

Elizabeth patted her pillow. "Do you want to try to go back to sleep?"

Juliana nodded.

"We'll be right downstairs if you need us, OK?" Amy said, turning off the overhead light.

"OK. Good night!" Juliana responded, sliding underneath her red quilt.

"We'll see you on Friday," Elizabeth said. "Good night." She got up and started to head out of the room.

"Elizabeth?" Juliana called softly.

Elizabeth paused in the doorway, concerned. "What is it?"

"Don't forget to get dressed tomorrow!" Juliana yelled, then dived under the covers, muffling her laughter.

Five

◇

"Hi, Mr. Karsten. I'm Winston Egbert, from the Five Friends Baby-sitting Service," Winston said, standing on the Karstens' welcome mat Thursday evening. He was proud of himself for actually showing up ten minutes early. It was his first baby-sitting job, and he planned on getting everything right. *That way, I'll get the money I have to have by Monday. I'll need every last—and first—penny!*

"Yes, Winston. We've been expecting you." Mr. Karsten stepped aside. He was a tall man, and he was wearing a dark gray, very expensive-looking suit. "Come on in and meet the twins!" he said cheerfully.

"Oh, hello there, Winston!" Mrs. Karsten called out from the kitchen. "I'm just making sure the twins have enough clean bottles ready."

"Bottles. Right," Winston said, standing in the kitchen doorway. "Of course, baby bottles."

Mrs. Karsten was wearing a shiny blue dress and black patent pumps. She had on a lot of jewelry, too. Their house was in one of the nicest sections of town. *These people look rich. I bet they'll pay me ten dollars an hour!* Winston thought, grinning happily at his new employers.

"Let's see . . . as you know, the juice should be fed to them at room temperature, milk should be warmed if you need to get them to sleep, and of course, water, whenever they want it, is fine . . . and there's plenty of soda in the fridge for you. Help yourself. Here's our phone number for the evening, plus the number of the twins' doctor, and my neighbor, and—"

"Relax, honey," Mr. Karsten said. "Winston looks like an old pro. He can figure everything out for himself. Can't you, Winston?"

"I'm sure I'll have everything completely under control," Winston confidently replied. "Piece of cake." He glanced around the kitchen counter. Speaking of cake . . . where was all the great food baby-sitters were supposed to get?

"There are some leftovers from dinner in the fridge. You can heat them up in the microwave. You know how to use a microwave, don't you?" Mrs. Karsten asked. "Remember, don't put metal in it, or plates that aren't microwave safe."

"Oh, I know all about microwaves," Winston

said. "Practically enough to write a book."

Mr. Karsten clapped him on the back. "I have a good feeling about you already, Winston. I'm sure the twins will be safe with you for the next few hours."

"Safe—and perfectly happy," Winston assured him. "Sir." In Winston's experience, it never hurt to throw that word in from time to time.

"Well, your mother told me that you're very reliable when I asked her for a quick reference yesterday. She also told me that you're not available Saturdays because you're learning to play the accordion. How wonderful!" Mrs. Karsten said.

"Mm," Winston mumbled. Wonderful wasn't the word he would have used, but if it made Mrs. Karsten happy, it couldn't be a bad thing.

"Wow. Not a lot of kids your age take up the accordion," Mr. Karsten said, giving Winston a puzzled look.

"Yes, I know," Winston said. *And that's the problem! That's why I'm here in the first place!* Not that he didn't like kids—in fact, he really loved playing with them. He just wouldn't have been as eager if it weren't for his debt to Charlie, that was all. "Well, the accordion's just one of my many interests. See, I'm into trying things no one else does. I mean, everyone plays the guitar, right?" he told Mr. Karsten.

"You don't follow trends, you set them?" Mr. Karsten asked.

"Exactly," Winston said. "Now if only I can get the accordion to be trendy. . . ."

Mr. Karsten laughed. "Good luck!"

"We'll be home as close to nine o'clock as possible," Mrs. Karsten said. "The twins just had dinner, but they may need a snack a bit later. Cheerios are fine or applesauce. Give them their pacifiers if they make a fuss. Extra diapers are on the changing table in their room, pink for Karla, blue for Kevin . . . let's see, have I forgotten anything?" She refastened one of her earrings and turned to her husband.

"Well . . . where exactly *are* the twins right now?" Winston asked, looking around the large living room.

"Oh, *I'm* sorry. Listen to me, going on and on about them without even introducing you!" Mrs. Karsten groaned.

"You're just overwhelmed, honey—don't worry. I was about to show Winston the nursery anyhow," Mr. Karsten said. As they walked down the hall he shook his head. "Confidentially, Winston, sometimes I think that staying home all day with the twins is too hard on her. I wonder if you could help out some afternoons, maybe—give her a chance to get out by herself, take walks . . ."

"That sounds like a very good idea," Winston agreed. He was going to become the richest babysitter in Sweet Valley if things worked out. After he paid off Charlie, he could start saving for that drum set he wanted, and then . . .

"Here we are," Mr. Karsten whispered as they

reached the nursery. "The twins have just gone down for a short nap after dinner. They may wake up while we're gone, and they may not. Who knows, you might be watching TV the whole time!"

Winston nodded, staring at the small bundles in two identical cribs. "They're adorable," he murmured, looking at their rosy red cheeks. They were so tiny! So cute! And their faces looked so sweet and peaceful. He couldn't wait to pick them up, tickle them, and hold them. This job was going to be a cinch!

After the Karstens left, Winston leaped onto the couch, a bag of cheese popcorn in his hand. He propped his feet on the coffee table and dug the remote out from between two cushions.

This is the life, he thought. *Just me, an unlimited supply of snacks, and a Lakers game.* He couldn't picture a better way to spend a Thursday night. And when it was all over, he'd be at least ten bucks richer than he was at that very moment. Just for hanging out at someone else's house in case a cute little baby—or two—needed him!

Why didn't I check out this baby-sitting thing before? he wondered. "Yes!" he whispered as a Lakers guard hit a long three-point shot.

At that exact moment a very loud, teeth-rattling clap of thunder rumbled through the air. Rain started pouring heavily on the roof. Within seconds it was streaming down the windows while lightning flashed and thunder boomed.

From the nursery came two ear-piercing wails.

Winston laughed nervously. "I guess Karla and Kevin don't like thunderstorms."

The twins screeched again, this time even louder. Winston felt like covering his ears. He'd never heard such noise in his life! Their cries made the thunder seem like a faint, distant rumble in comparison.

Winston glanced at the closed front door. Was it too late to ask the Karstens to stay home for the night? He rushed to the window just in time to see their red Ford Explorer pull away from the curb.

Uh-oh. Maybe baby-sitting wasn't going to be a cinch after all. But the storm had to stop sometime, didn't it? he thought, panicking as he rushed down the hall to the nursery. That's what thunderstorms do, he consoled himself. They start, and they stop. They came, they went. They stormed, they calmed.

But did the same scientific principle work for screaming babies? Winston wondered, stepping into the nursery.

Elizabeth hurried down the sidewalk Thursday evening, glancing nervously at the sky. One section of it was completely dark, and a large black cloud looked like it was about to pour with rain. She only had a few more blocks to go before she reached the downtown movie theater.

Since she had the night off from baby-sitting, she and her friend Maria Slater had decided to catch the six-fifteen show. *Looks like I'll make it just in time,* Elizabeth thought as the air rumbled with thunder.

She was walking past the pet store when a figure stepped out from a doorway, directly blocking her path and looming over her.

"Hey, what are you—" Elizabeth looked up, frightened, her heart beating quickly. Then something clicked. This was no stranger—it was Mr. Brangwen, almost knocking her down again! "What are *you* doing here?" she asked.

The Riccolis' gardener coughed, his lungs wheezing as if he'd just been running. "I was . . . I had . . . ," he gasped. "Never mind, it is not important," he finally said in his deep voice, fixing Elizabeth with a stern gaze.

Then why do I get the creepy feeling that you were just following me? Elizabeth wondered. "Well, I'm in a hurry," she said, starting to walk off. "I have to meet a friend right now and—"

"The important thing is that I have run into you," Mr. Brangwen continued, as if Elizabeth hadn't spoken at all. "There is something I must tell you tonight."

Elizabeth stepped under the pet store awning as it started to rain. What could he possibly have to tell her? "Um . . . why tonight?" she asked.

"Because I did not see you last night. But I wanted to warn you as soon as possible!" he said ominously.

Elizabeth fidgeted with the strap on her umbrella. "Warn me? About what?" She wondered if he was going to mention not closing her eyes again. Or not leaving her bike in the wrong place. She stifled a giggle as she remembered Jessica calling Mr. Brangwen the "hedge police."

"About the Sullivan mansion." Mr. Brangwen stepped closer to Elizabeth and whispered conspiratorially. "Be very careful! Or she'll get you in your sleep!"

"She?" Elizabeth asked, confused. Who was he talking about? And why was he still calling it the Sullivan mansion? He worked for the Riccoli family now.

"Yes," Mr. Brangwen said, nodding. "She'll get you in your sleep. She'll—"

A tremendously loud crack of thunder split the air. Mr. Brangwen looked up at the sky as a bolt of lightning flashed.

It's now or never, Elizabeth told herself. *And I'm getting out of here now!* She took off for the movie theater, popping open her umbrella as she ran. She had to get away from Mr. Brangwen—he was too weird!

"Wait—stop!" Mr. Brangwen shouted. "I have more to tell you! I have to—" His voice was drowned out by the pouring rain.

Elizabeth reached the end of the block and darted left, taking a shortcut to the theater. She definitely wasn't going to stand around in a dark, raging thunderstorm talking to someone as creepy as Mr. Brangwen.

What was he talking about? What was so important? "She'll get you," he had said. Who was "she"? And why would Mr. Brangwen bother following Elizabeth around town just to deliver an ominous warning?

Elizabeth had a feeling that Mr. Brangwen had let all the haunted rumors get to him over the years. Either that or he'd spent too much time gardening in the bright sun. Anyone who did the gardening at a haunted, abandoned house for twenty-five years had to be a little strange.

Anyway, it didn't make sense. If there was something bizarre or dangerous happening at the old Sullivan mansion . . . why would Mr. Brangwen still work there?

Elizabeth shivered as she stepped into the theater lobby. Whatever Mr. Brangwen was talking about . . . that was the last she wanted to hear of it!

"OK," Winston told himself. "Focus."

He stared at the babies, who were perched in identical high chairs, facing each other and screeching at the top of their lungs. *They're only eight months old*, Winston thought. *So how can they be so loud? Don't lungs develop slowly like . . . height?*

"I'm sure the twins will be safe with you," Mr. Karsten had said. *But what about me being safe with them?* Winston despaired. "If they make a fuss," Mrs. Karsten told him. *If! How about when, and how often!* They hadn't stopped in the forty-five minutes since the Karstens had left.

Winston had tried everything: singing to them, playing their favorite movie, cradling them in his arms while he danced around. . . . And they had stopped crying . . . for a few seconds. And then they had started up again, even louder than before. Winston was running out of ideas.

All of a sudden he remembered Mrs. Karsten's instructions. Winston snapped his fingers. "You guys want something to drink, don't you? You're thirsty, right? Hey, I know how that feels. I'm absolutely parched!" Winston clutched his throat and staggered around the kitchen. "I'm dying of thirst, I'm dying! Hold on a second, OK?" He smiled nervously at the twins, and they stopped yelling.

Finally! He opened the refrigerator and stared at the contents. Now, which beverage was it he was supposed to give them? Cold milk, warm juice, ice water . . . ginger ale? Definitely not coffee—they had more than enough energy already. Didn't babies like to sleep a lot, or was that just a rumor?

He poured a few cups of milk into a saucepan on the stove and set it on high. If warm milk made people sleepy, then hot milk would put the babies into slumberland in no time. Then Winston could settle onto the couch for some serious vegetating in front of the TV. "It's a plan," he muttered happily to himself.

That was when he noticed it. A certain very unpleasant smell. *No. Please, no,* he told himself. But he knew there was no getting around it. It was time to confront the diapers.

"OK, which one of you needs to be changed?" He stared at Karla and then at Kevin. "Who am I kidding. They're *twins*. They both need to be changed." He shook his head and went over to the high chairs, carefully unfastening Kevin and then Karla. Then he picked them up one at a time, cradling one in his left arm and one in his right. Making a face, he dashed down the hall to the nursery.

"OK. You guys just lie there and I'll . . ." Winston stared at the diaper box on the changing table. "Read the directions."

Actually, it wasn't the first time he'd changed diapers in his life. He had done some baby-sitting before, and he had seen a lot of diaper commercials on TV. It didn't take him too long to whisk the twins into new diapers. In fact, as he fastened the tabs, pulling them tightly so there'd be no gaps, he thought he'd done an even *better* job than the Karstens themselves.

Then he noticed that he'd put the pink diaper on Kevin and the blue one on Karla. "Well, you guys are probably tired of all those baby stereotypes anyway, right?" he joked. "Who says you can't have your own identities?"

He sniffed the air. The babies were all freshly powdered . . . so what was that obnoxious, burning— "The milk!" Winston cried, leaving the babies on their changing table for a second as he ran down the hallway.

The milk had evaporated, burning to the bottom of the pan. "So much for a hot drink," he moaned. But at least the twins had stopped crying. He turned off the stove and put the pan in the sink.

Then he collected Karla and Kevin from the nursery

and put them in their playpen in the living room. He clicked on the television. *Now everything's going to be calm and relaxed,* he told himself. *The way it's supposed to be.*

"How about some soda?" he offered the babies. "I know I want a cola." Karla waved a rattle at him. "I'll take that for a yes, little lady!" He winked at Karla, and she squealed happily.

Winston poured the soda into two bottles, then poured himself a glassful. He went over to the playpen and handed each baby a bottle. Karla took a few sips and put her bottle down in the playpen, more interested in playing with a yellow stuffed elephant. Kevin waved his bottle in the air.

"Easy, Kevin—you're supposed to drink it, like this!" Winston lifted his glass to his mouth and made loud, gulping noises. He rubbed his stomach. "Mm, mm, good."

Kevin giggled, then threw his bottle flat against the wall. The top popped off, and soda exploded out of the bottle! Winston watched as the brown, sticky stuff streamed down the white paint and splattered onto the floral couch. His heart caught in his throat. This was a disaster!

The twins erupted into squeals of laughter.

"Sure, it's funny to you," Winston muttered, running to get a roll of paper towels. But their parents, who were due home in half an hour, probably wouldn't find much to laugh at.

Six

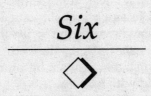

"Mom! It's Mrs. Riccoli!" Jessica called excitedly down the stairs Thursday night. She answered the phone, expecting a call from Lila. But instead it was an interior-decorating call from Mrs. Riccoli. This was even better!

"OK, I'll take it in the den!" Mrs. Wakefield called up to Jessica.

Jessica put her ear up against the phone, staying on the line. "Mrs. Riccoli, I'm still here—you know, in case you want my help, too. Since I've seen your house and everything." She grinned, admiring her good business sense.

"That's fine," Mrs. Riccoli said.

"Hello? Mrs. Riccoli? This is Alice Wakefield. How are you?" Jessica's mother asked.

"Well, I've got my hands full tonight as usual, but I

wanted to at least give you a call and touch base," Mrs. Riccoli said. "Jessica's told me so much about you."

"She's told me a lot about you, too," Mrs. Wakefield said. "Welcome to Sweet Valley!"

"Thanks. I don't feel quite settled yet, but I'm starting to. As Jessica's probably already told you, I'd like to get some work done on the interior of our house. The upstairs is fine, the bedrooms and so forth. But downstairs . . . it's a bit of a nightmare," Mrs. Riccoli said with a laugh.

"It's not that bad!" Jessica said. Of course, it *was* that bad, but Jessica knew it was important to act professional in these situations. "You just need to make the . . . what's the word when you change from like a small house to a big, kind of fancy house?"

"Transition?" her mother suggested.

"Right," Jessica said. "It's just that the style of their *old* furniture doesn't really go with their *new* house." *Like, at all.* "It's time to make the transition."

"With five kids keeping me busy, I haven't had time to think about doing much of anything," Mrs. Riccoli said. "But I was wondering if you could help me, Mrs. Wakefield."

"I'd love to," Mrs. Wakefield said. "And please, call me Alice. How about if we set up a short meeting at your house, and we'll talk about what you have in mind. We can share some ideas, and then I'll start looking for things you might like."

"Oh, that sounds wonderful—and easy. And please call me Christina. The only problem is . . . finding a quiet time for us to talk," Mrs. Riccoli said.

"I know!" Jessica said excitedly. "I'll go with you, Mom. That way I can watch all the kids while *you* guys talk. And you don't even have to pay me, Mrs. Riccoli—it's free!" Not that Jessica would usually work at anything for free . . . but she figured if her mother took the job, she'd have more money to spread around. And maybe she'd start by raising Jessica's allowance.

"You'll baby-sit for free?" Mrs. Riccoli laughed. "Well, *that's* an offer I can't refuse. Interior decorating and baby-sitting all in one visit! How does next Wednesday sound to you both? Jessica comes to baby-sit that night, so you could just come by with her an hour early, say, at five o'clock? I'm afraid that I'm really too busy to set aside any real time until then."

"Sounds perfect, Christina. And where's your house?" Mrs. Wakefield asked.

Just then Jessica heard Andrew yell in the background, "Give me that toy right now or I'll pound you!"

"Stop! Mom, make him stop!" Jessica heard Gretchen shriek.

"Oh dear. I'd better go," Mrs. Riccoli said quickly. "Video game emergency."

"It's OK—I know how to get there, Mom," Jessica said.

"See you next Wednesday!" Mrs. Riccoli said, sounding harried.

Jessica hung up the phone and collapsed on her

bed with a sigh. She was too helpful for words. And if her mother wanted to give her a commission for finding her the work . . . or Mrs. Riccoli wanted to pay Jessica extra for her baby-sitting time because she found her a decorator? Jessica wouldn't say no. Being selfless was OK. Just not *all* the time.

Mr. and Mrs. Karsten tiptoed into the house. "Winston! How did it go?" Mrs. Karsten asked in a soft voice. She looked nervously at him.

"Fine!" Winston said with a casual shrug. He plucked the last piece of burnt milk skin off the bottom of the pan. He soaped the saucepan one more time, then rinsed the pan and put it in the dish drainer. "Just perfect. They're absolute dolls!" *And I'm lying through my teeth!*

"Oh, that's wonderful." Mrs. Karsten clasped her hands together and smiled. "I was so worried!"

"See? Everything's fine, just like I said it would be," Mr. Karsten assured his wife.

"So they're sleeping?" Mrs. Karsten asked.

Winston nodded. "Like, well, like babies." In fact, the twins were sleeping so peacefully, it was hard to believe they'd made his life miserable for two hours and forty-five minutes straight. Feeding them those Cheerios and bowls of cherry Jell-O had worked like a charm; after their stomachs were full, they were zonked.

Mr. Karsten laughed, clapping Winston on the back. "I told you—they probably slept the whole time, didn't they?"

Winston bit his lip. "Just about, I'd say!" *Of course, I could also say that they were awake and screaming the whole time, but I won't!* Winston just wanted to get his money and get out the door. He cleared his throat. "Well, I should get going—my parents want me home by nine-fifteen."

"All right. Let's see . . . five dollars an hour, three hours—here's fifteen dollars." Mrs. Karsten opened her wallet and handed Winston three five-dollar bills.

Winston stared at the money. *That's it?* he thought. *Three hours of nonstop tortured suffering for fifteen lousy bucks?* Of course, five bucks an hour was the going rate, according to Elizabeth—for one baby, anyway. But if that was true, shouldn't twin babies rate *ten* dollars?

Then he remembered Charlie Cashman. Charlie wanted twenty-five, and this would be more than half. It was a start, anyway. "Great, thanks," Winston said, shoving the money into his pocket. "Hey, this was fun. If you ever need another baby-sitter . . ." *Like in the next three days, before I have to come up with the rest of the money for Charlie?* "Call me!" Winston said.

"Will do," Mr. Karsten said, nodding.

That was when Winston noticed it. A big glob of cherry Jell-O hanging from the ceiling, right above Mr. Karsten's head. Winston sucked in his breath. Any second now it was going to drop and slime Mr. Karsten.

"G-good night!" Winston said, quickly closing the door.

*   *   *

"Can you imagine having a class on a Friday night? I wonder if anyone even shows up," Todd said. "Let's see . . . should I go to History 101 or a movie? Gee, what a tough call."

"It would be hard, especially after classes all week," Elizabeth agreed. She and Todd were baby-sitting at the Riccolis' house. It was the third night that week for Elizabeth—she was really starting to feel at home there. Even if it was a little strange to be hanging out with Todd on Friday night, kind of like it was a date. A date—with five kids attached!

"When I go to college, I'm picking my classes based on when they're held," Todd continued. "No Monday morning classes ever again! Yes!" He pumped his fist into the air.

Elizabeth laughed. "Not even if it was a class you really, really wanted to take? Something you needed for your major?"

"Hm. Well . . . I guess I could always change my major," Todd said. "It's only my life, right?" He and Elizabeth started laughing even harder when suddenly a cry filtered down from upstairs.

"Help! Help me!"

"What was that—," Todd began.

"It's Juliana," Elizabeth said, tossing the magazine off her lap as she stood up. *Not again!* "She has bad nightmares—come on!"

The two of them hurried upstairs. Elizabeth had been so relieved when Juliana dropped right off to sleep earlier that evening. She'd assumed that the little girl was no longer having bad dreams. Juliana hadn't mentioned them once in conversation that night and neither had Mrs. Riccoli. Juliana looked well rested and happy, as if she'd been sleeping fine.

Maybe it only happens the nights I'm here. Maybe I'm a jinx! Elizabeth thought.

She rushed into Juliana's room and quickly woke her. "Juliana, it's me, Elizabeth. And Todd's right here. Nobody's going to hurt you."

Juliana woke up and clutched Elizabeth tightly, her body racked with sobs. "Make her stop! Make her go away!"

"Hey, it's OK," Todd said, sitting on the bed. "Elizabeth and I are watching out for you." He turned to Elizabeth. "Who's she talking about?" he mouthed.

Elizabeth let go of Juliana so that she could hand her a tissue. There was something about these nightmares that was really starting to worry her. "There's this girl who keeps showing up in her dreams. Right, Juliana?"

Juliana had calmed down a little bit. She angrily brushed the tears off her face. "It's a horrible mean girl, and I hate her!" she declared.

"I know," Elizabeth said, putting her hand on Juliana's arm. "But she's going to leave you alone soon, I promise." All of a sudden Mr. Brangwen's warning of the night before flashed into her mind: "She'll get you in your sleep." Did Mr. Brangwen have the same nightmare about somebody trying to hurt him? Or was he the one who'd scared Juliana in the first place? If he felt strongly enough about it to warn Elizabeth, who didn't even live at the house, was it possible that he'd tried to warn Juliana in the same way?

"What do you think is going on?" Todd whispered. "You told me she's had these bad dreams every night you've been here."

Elizabeth nodded. She and Todd were standing in the doorway to Juliana's bedroom, watching to make sure she was all right. They'd stayed with her until she finally fell back asleep. "I'm not sure, but I might have an idea. At first I thought she was having nightmares because she just moved. But there's that gardener, Mr. Brangwen—"

"The grumpy, mean guy? The one who yelled at you and Jessica about your bikes?" Todd asked.

"Yeah. But that's not all he did. Last night he gave me this weird warning. He even tracked me down, downtown—as if he were following me," Elizabeth said. A shiver ran through her. Just remembering Mr. Brangwen on that dark, rainy street gave her goose bumps. He *had* followed her. The more she thought about it, the more it made sense to her.

"You're kidding," Todd breathed.

Elizabeth shook her head. "It was in the middle of that thunderstorm, which made it even more scary. He said I should be careful here because she could get me in my sleep," she explained in a whisper.

"Todd, he said I shouldn't close my eyes. And that's what Juliana thinks—that she can't close her eyes or the girl's going to get her!" She clutched Todd's arm.

"But Elizabeth . . . come on, I know you're scared. But that's ridiculous. There's no such thing as some-body *getting* you in your sleep." Todd frowned. "That guy's full of hot air! He's just using the power of suggestion to scare you guys."

"The power of suggestion," Elizabeth repeated. She glanced down at her hand on Todd's arm and withdrew it, feeling embarrassed. Was she getting carried away over nothing? "So you think he said the same scary things to Juliana and that's why she's having bad dreams?"

Todd nodded. "It has to be that. See, you're older, so if Mr. Brangwen says something like that to you, you know he's just making stuff up. But Juliana's too young—she doesn't realize he's only trying to scare her."

Elizabeth's brow furrowed. It was true—she was older, and she *did* think Mr. Brangwen was making things up. At least, she used to think that way—now she wasn't so sure. "I guess that makes sense. But why does Mr. Brangwen want to scare her?" Elizabeth asked Todd. "Or me?"

"Maybe he doesn't want anyone to live here," Todd said. "Maybe he likes being the gardener at an abandoned house for some weird reason."

"He is kind of weird," Elizabeth said. "But . . . you really don't think there's any truth to what he said?"

"Elizabeth!" Todd stared at her. "Don't tell me you're actually getting caught up in this whole thing. You don't believe there's actually anything going on to be worried about, do you?"

"Oh . . . no, not really," Elizabeth said. "But I am worried about Juliana. She can't keep having these nightmares!"

"Then I think you ought to have a little talk with Mr. Brangwen," Todd said. "Tell him to stop putting those creepy ideas in her head."

"Yeah, I guess I could." Elizabeth knew Todd was right. She had to talk to Mr. Brangwen. But she didn't want to see him again. The two times she'd already talked to him were bad enough.

Why did he want to scare all of them, anyway?

Seven

"Well, if it isn't Mr. Polka." Charlie leaned his hand against Winston's locker Monday morning, slamming the door shut. "Heard any good tunes lately? Or are you too busy practicing your scales, Egghead?"

Winston smiled nervously. *Stall, Winston. Stall,* he told himself. "I didn't see you at Mr. Pagnowski's on Saturday. Are you giving up the guitar?" Winston asked.

"Ha," Charlie replied. "No way."

"Really? You're a man of excellent, refined taste," Winston said, putting his hand on Charlie's shoulder. "I thought maybe you heard me playing last week and you decided to ditch the guitar for the accordion, which is a good call. We could play some duets—"

"Yeah, right. Listen, Egbert. Don't touch me."

Charlie shook his shoulder, throwing off Winston's hand. "I don't want to chat about music. I just want the money so I can go buy some new CDs after school today," Charlie said. "So hand it over already."

"You know how much I'd love to. But the thing is . . . the thing is . . ."

"What *is* the thing?" Charlie demanded impatiently.

"Well, I . . . I can't," Winston said.

Charlie glared at him. "What do you mean, you *can't*?" He made it sound like the word wasn't even in the English language.

"Well, you're, um, leaning against my locker, and the money's inside," Winston explained. *Ha! Got you on that one*, he thought.

"Oh." Charlie stepped back, looking almost disappointed that he didn't have a reason to beat up Winston.

Winston opened his locker, got out his knapsack, and pulled his wallet out of the outside pocket. *Think fast*, he told himself. *The main idea here is to stall until the first bell. And the second. And the third.* He turned to Charlie and smiled. "You know about loans and financing, right?"

Charlie gave him a confused stare. "What, are you going to pay me with a credit card?"

"Exactly!" Winston said. "Well, not exactly, but close. You've heard of installment plans? Like when you buy a house and you make a down payment, but then every month—"

Charlie slammed the locker door shut again.

"Egbert, hand over the twenty-five bucks. *Now.*"

"Right. Of course." Winston opened his wallet and pulled out the three five-dollar bills. He placed them in Charlie's palm. *If he notices that's not enough, he's better in math than I thought.* "There you go," he said.

Charlie frowned, counting each bill. "Egbert, that's only fifteen. I said twenty-five. Give me the other ten bucks."

"Oh . . . is that only fifteen? But—wait! I had twenty-five this morning. I've been robbed!" Winston cried, looking desperately around the hall for a teacher. "You know, you just *cannot* leave anything valuable in your locker these days."

Charlie stared at Winston, stuffed the money in his pocket, and folded his arms across his chest. "I don't care why you only have fifteen bucks for me. And I don't have time for any more of your dumb stalling tactics. But if you don't get me the other ten by, say . . . Wednesday—"

"Wednesday?" Winston gulped. "But today's Monday!"

"Good. You can count the days," Charlie sneered, grabbing Winston's collar. "That means you'll be able to count all the way up to fifteen. Either give me fifteen dollars on Wednesday or your little polka-playing hobby will be all over school."

"F-fifteen?" Winston sputtered.

"Finance charges. You know," Charlie said, releasing Winston. "See you Wednesday."

Winston slumped against his locker. Ten, fifteen . . . what did it matter? He didn't have a chance!

Maybe there's a school I can transfer to where accordions and polkas are cool, he thought.

"I don't know what to do, Amy. Juliana just doesn't seem to be getting over this like we thought she would," Elizabeth said on Monday. She and Amy were eating lunch in the cafeteria. They were both going to baby-sit for the Riccolis' that night.

"Have you told Mrs. Riccoli about it yet?" Amy asked.

"I mentioned it once, but she didn't seem to think it was that important," Elizabeth said.

Amy looked surprised. "Maybe you should talk it over with her again. Maybe she wasn't aware of how often they happen."

Elizabeth nodded. She knew she ought to discuss Juliana's bad dreams again with her mother, but Mrs. Riccoli was always so busy. "I guess I was kind of hoping that I could solve Juliana's problems by myself. That way I wouldn't have to bother her again. And I feel like I'm so close to figuring it out! Remember how the gardener warned me about not closing my eyes?" Elizabeth asked, putting down her turkey sandwich.

Amy nodded. "And scared you half to death by following you in the middle of a thunderstorm?"

"Right," Elizabeth said. "Well, Todd and I were talking the other night—"

"Mm-hm. I bet," Amy teased. She winked at Elizabeth.

"*Anyway*, as I was saying," Elizabeth continued, trying not to blush. "I think that maybe Mr. Brangwen gave Juliana the same kind of warning, and that's why she's so frightened."

"Could be," Amy remarked. She tapped the table with her fingers. "That guy is pretty weird. I mean, someone who takes care of a garden at an *abandoned* house has to have at least a couple of screws loose."

"Well, I'm not sure about that. But it's almost like . . . I don't know. Like he doesn't want the Riccolis to live there, so he's trying to scare them—and us—away," Elizabeth said.

"With a bunch of creepy stories and warnings?" Amy shrugged, opening up a package of chocolate cookies. "Makes sense to me. But why doesn't he want anyone living there?"

"Maybe he's worked there so long, he feels like it's his house," Elizabeth suggested.

"Where does he live, anyway?" Amy asked. "I mean, does he have one of those servants' quarters kind of things on the property?"

Elizabeth pictured the Riccoli house and its surrounding grounds. "No, there's nothing like that. He must live in town somewhere."

"Oh. Well, maybe our theory's not right, then." Amy bit into a cookie. "But in any case, the next time I see him, I'm going to tell him to stop bugging Juliana with those weird stories."

"I feel like going over there right after school and telling him to lay off before he can say anything else to Juliana," Elizabeth said, determined. "But my family's having this special early dinner at five, and I have to help get it ready."

"Really? What's the dinner for?" Amy asked.

"Oh, my mom wants to celebrate because she picked up three new decorating jobs last week. One of them is to redo Mrs. Riccoli's house—isn't that exciting?" Elizabeth said.

"Cool," Amy said. "So your mom's probably going to be over there as much as you are. And you know what that means."

"No, what?" Elizabeth asked.

"No more riding our bikes! Which could come in handy since there have been all those thunderstorms lately," Amy said. "I bet Mr. Brangwen is going nuts, with the wind damaging his precious hedges."

"Better the wind than our bikes," Elizabeth said with a smile, trying her best to push Mr. Brangwen and his strange warning out of her head. There was nothing she could do about *him* until tonight, when she went to the Riccolis' house.

I'll just have to speak to him. He has to tell Juliana he made up all those stories and that there's nothing to be afraid of.

Because Juliana can't keep living in fear of her dreams.

"We're having the most deluxe dinner," Jessica announced to Lila on the telephone Monday afternoon.

"Steak, baked potatoes, corn on the cob, salad, and this unbelievable-looking cherry pie that my mom made last night."

She decided not to mention that at that very moment, she was supposed to be in the kitchen helping prepare the meal. When her mother had asked her to chop vegetables, she'd suddenly remembered that she urgently needed to call Lila about a homework assignment. A homework assignment on . . . gossiping.

"Sounds great. What's the occasion?" Lila asked.

"The occasion is that my mom's decorating business is booming," Jessica said, punching the cushion behind her on the couch. "Thanks to me."

"You?" Lila sounded skeptical. "What did you do?"

"I started it all," Jessica replied breezily. "I got my mother on this incredible roll just by recommending her to Mrs. Riccoli, that woman we've been baby-sitting for."

"The one with the striped vinyl beanbag chairs?" Lila asked in a snooty tone.

"Right. Her," Jessica said. "But Lila, you know, you shouldn't judge someone just on the basis of their furniture."

"You're the one who told me how horrible those chairs were!" Lila protested.

"Anyway," Jessica continued. If Lila didn't want to admit that she was a snob, Jessica couldn't force her. "She's a professor at Sweet Valley University, and she mentioned my mom to a couple of other professors there, and now Mom's going to do some redecorating for them, too!"

"Wow. You probably won't see her again, she'll be so busy," Lila commented. "I personally wouldn't want to work that hard." She sighed. "Fortunately I'll never have to."

"Well, aren't you lucky." Jessica rolled her eyes. Lila couldn't understand that for some people, like her mother, working was actually fun. "Anyway," she went on, "I was thinking that since her thriving business really *is* all due to me, maybe she'll give me a cut of the profits. You know, like a Hollywood agent—when they find work for actors, they get to keep a percentage or whatever."

"Jessica. Come back to earth," Lila said. "Your mother wouldn't do that in a million years."

Jessica frowned. "Well, if she makes a lot of money—"

"A bunch of professors aren't going to spend that much," Lila broke in. "Anyway, aren't you earning a lot working for the Riccolis?"

"Yeah!" Jessica said, her mood brightening a little. "I was there on Saturday and Sunday, watching the kids while Mrs. Riccoli went shopping."

"So what do you need any extra money for?" Lila asked. "Isn't that enough?"

Jessica sighed. As if Lila had any idea about how much money was "enough"! She only had everything she wanted and more, and she'd never had to work a day in her life. "Lila, isn't it you who's always saying you can never have enough?"

"Yes, that's true," Lila said.

"So what do you think?" Jessica pressed. "Would it be totally out of line if I asked my mother for a cut of the profits?"

Lila giggled. "Maybe she'll give you Mrs. Riccoli's old furniture!"

"Ha ha," Jessica muttered. "You're really funny, Lila." *But when I have as much money as you do, you won't think it's such a riot!*

"Is this Winston?"

Winston gulped. The voice on the other end of the phone was Mr. Karsten's. *The Jell-O,* he thought. *It stained the ceiling beyond repair. It fell on his head and blinded him. No—the saucepan! They couldn't get rid of the burnt milk smell. Or . . . wait! The twins won't drink anything but soda.* He took a deep breath to collect himself. "Y-yes?" he replied.

"This is Ben Karsten. How's it going, Winston?" he said cheerfully.

Winston let out a sigh. It didn't sound like Mr. Karsten was calling to yell at him. Then again, adults could be pretty sneaky about things like that. They were nice and then—wham! They got you with the old one-two punch of criticism. Winston ought to know; he'd been to the principal's office enough times for clowning around in class to qualify for the Sweet Valley Middle School Hall of Fame.

"Hi, Mr. Karsten," Winston said nervously. "I'm . . . OK, I guess. How are you?"

"Great," Mr. Karsten replied. "Thanks again for helping us out the other night. We had a great evening, thanks to you."

Winston smiled uneasily. "Happy to help." *Kind of. At least, when I wasn't changing diapers.*

"I'm calling because I was wondering if you could baby-sit for us again," Mr. Karsten said.

Winston almost dropped the phone. "You're kidding," he muttered. Then he cleared his throat. "I mean, really?"

"We definitely want you back. We were hoping you'd be available tomorrow night," Mr. Karsten said. "I realize it's kind of short notice, but if there's *any* way you could manage it, we'd be very grateful."

Any way I can manage it? Winston thought. Was Mr. Karsten kidding? There was no way he *couldn't* manage it, not with Charlie breathing down his neck for that extra ten—make it fifteen—dollars! "That sounds fine. I'm definitely free," Winston happily told Mr. Karsten. "When do you need me?"

"From five to eight," Mr. Karsten said.

"Perfect!" Winston cried. Three hours equaled fifteen dollars, at least. "I mean, that sounds fine. I'll be there!"

"Great. See you then, Winston."

After Mr. Karsten hung up, Winston put down the phone and pumped his fist into the air. "Yes!" Now he would get the money to Charlie by

Wednesday, just like he was supposed to, and his problems would be all over. He could go back to living a normal life and—

"Wait a second," Winston said out loud. Did he just *happily* agree to take care of those nightmare twins for another three hours? He'd barely made it through the first night with them, and he'd spent an hour cleaning up the messes they'd made in a mere five minutes.

But then Winston pictured Charlie, holding him by the collar in front of his locker. There was really no question. He had to go back to the Karstens.

He was about to head downstairs for dinner when the phone rang again. *Please don't be Mr. Karsten calling to cancel!* he thought, picking up the receiver. "Hello?"

"Egghead. It's me, Charlie."

Winston grinned. He had nothing to be afraid of now that he knew he'd get Charlie his money after all. "Hello, Charlie! What's up?"

"What's up is that I want to know if you have that extra fifteen dollars yet," Charlie replied. "Because if you don't . . . it's oom-pah-pah for your reputation." He snickered.

"For your information it's not a tuba, it's an accordion. And besides, you said Wednesday, and I'll get it to you on Wednesday," Winston said casually. "No problem!"

"What time Wednesday?" Charlie asked.

Talk about greedy! Winston thought. He'd have the money Tuesday night, but he didn't want to hand it over to Charlie until he absolutely had to. Winston might be an easy target for blackmail, but he was at least going to set *some* standards. "How about . . . sundown on Wednesday," he suggested, trying to be dramatic.

"Huh?" Charlie asked. "Do you mean, like, after school?"

Winston sighed. Drama was wasted on someone like Charlie Cashman. In fact, Charlie's last name was starting to take on a whole new meaning . . . as in, *Where's the cash, man?*

"Yeah," he told Charlie. "After school. Meet me at my house at about . . . five o'clock. I think I can have the money by then."

Charlie snorted. "You'd better do more than *think* you have it. Because if you don't—"

"I'll have it, OK?" Winston replied. "And please don't mention it again until I see you at my house on Wednesday. I don't want anyone at school to get suspicious."

"Your secret's safe with me, Egghead," Charlie said.

Yeah, right, Winston thought.

"Now, which polka were you planning on performing at our next pep rally?" Charlie laughed.

"See you Wednesday, Charlie." Winston hung up the phone. He couldn't wait to get Charlie Cashman out of his life! And thanks to Mr. and Mrs. Karsten, Winston wouldn't have to wait much longer.

Eight

◇

"Fantastic steak, Dad. You're like the master gas grill chef of Sweet Valley," Jessica told her father Monday evening at dinner, slicing another bite's worth of steak.

Steven just nodded, his mouth full. "Mm."

"Elizabeth, is yours all right?" Mr. Wakefield asked, turning to her.

"Oh, sure, Dad," Elizabeth said, sounding distracted. She was cutting her baked potato into pieces, but she had hardly eaten a thing.

Jessica raised an eyebrow at Elizabeth. *What's up with her?* she wondered. Elizabeth always had a big appetite, and she'd put a lot of work into their special dinner, too. "You're baby-sitting tonight, aren't you?" she asked Elizabeth, trying to bring her into the conversation.

Elizabeth nodded. "With Amy."

Jessica frowned. "I feel like everyone else is getting more hours there than I am. It's not fair. I'm the one who needs money the most!"

"Jessica, didn't you baby-sit all weekend? And you're going Wednesday with me," Mrs. Wakefield reminded her. "Isn't that enough?"

"No!" Steven cried, banging his fork down on the table. "I can never baby-sit enough! Give me babies, toddlers, screaming infants!"

Jessica glared at him. "As if you'd know what to do with *one* baby, never mind five kids."

"Well, sure. It's harder for me," Steven said, straightening the napkin in his lap. "After all, I'm not as in tune with babies as you are."

"In tune?" Jessica muttered. "What's that supposed to mean?"

Steven grabbed another roll out of the wicker basket on the table. "Nothing. It's just that it's probably easier for you to understand them, seeing as they're not much younger than you." He buttered the roll, laughing under his breath.

Jessica glared at him. "Oh, really? I would think you'd get along great with babies, actually. Do the words *infantile humor* mean anything to you?" She giggled, looking at Elizabeth.

Elizabeth gave her a faint smile.

What's with her? Jessica wondered. Elizabeth was always right there supporting her when she made fun of Steven. What was on her mind so much that she couldn't join in and help?

*   *   *

"OK, Kevvie, I think you can let go of my neck now." Winston tried to gently pry Kevin's fingers off his neck, where they were painfully gripping his skin. He'd never known that babies were so strong. He felt like he was in the death grip of the Storming Crusader, his favorite pro wrestler.

"Wawoo," Kevin shouted, pulling on Winston's skin.

"Owwie," Winston cried, trying to unclasp Kevin's grip a little more aggressively this time.

"Ya-ya!" In the giant playpen on the floor Karla squealed with excitement, like a spectator at a boxing match.

Winston felt like he was learning a new, strange language. *I've heard of the terrible twos. But what about the atrocious eight-month-olds? Or maybe I can call this Terrible Twosday. After all, there are two of them.*

Winston finally wriggled his way out of Kevin's grasp and was about to set him back into the playpen when Kevin flung his arm out, knocking a ceramic vase off the mantelpiece.

Not that, too! Winston reached out to grab the vase, nearly dropping Kevin. "Whoa—whoops!" he yelled, catching the vase with his right hand and Kevin with his left. *That was a close one. A little too close.* Winston was running out of energy to keep everything and everyone safe and sound.

He laughed nervously. "Guess all those baseball games really paid off in some excellent catching skills!

OK, now, you play with that green terry tiger of yours," he instructed Kevin, setting the baby carefully in the playpen. "And you, young lady—it's time for your flying lesson!" He picked up Karla and started playing airplane, swooping her through the air.

Karla threw out an arm and boxed him squarely on the chin. Then she kicked her feet in the air, sending a picture frame crashing onto the floor.

"OK! Sometimes pilots need a few more lessons before we can let them into the friendly skies," Winston told Karla, sitting down on the couch and putting her on his lap.

He looked up at the grandfather clock. The good news was at least *it* wasn't broken yet. He couldn't say the same for the clock beside the changing table or the music box hanging from Karla's crib. But the bad news was it was seven-thirty. The babies seemed nowhere near ready to fall asleep, and the Karstens would be home in half an hour. He still had to clean up, find some glue to repair some broken things, change the twins, and put them to bed.

"So who feels tired?" Winston smiled at Karla, who was chewing on her foot through the sock. "Karla, Mr. Sandman is coming for you!"

"Waa . . . na . . . da . . . na . . . woo!" Karla wailed.

"Ooo . . . na!" Kevin chimed in.

If you can't beat 'em, join 'em. "Wacka-nacka-boo-hoo-hoo-shamu!" Winston cried.

Both babies' faces crinkled up, their lips puckered,

and they burst out crying, screaming at the top of their lungs.

"Guess I don't know the language as well as I thought." Winston groaned. "Maybe I offended them in 'baby.'"

"Mrs. Riccoli, can I talk to you for a minute?" Elizabeth stood on the porch outside the house on Monday night. Amy was inside, helping all the kids get settled down to do their homework, and Mrs. Riccoli was about to leave for Sweet Valley University.

"What is it, Elizabeth?" Mrs. Riccoli asked, turning around on the sidewalk. "Is something wrong?" A look of concern crossed her face as she shifted her briefcase from one shoulder to the other.

Elizabeth hurried down the steps until she was standing in front of Mrs. Riccoli. "I don't want to alarm you. But I'm kind of worried about Juliana."

"Juliana? Why?" Mrs. Riccoli asked.

"You know the nightmares she's been having? I mentioned them to you the other day, and you said not to worry," Elizabeth said. "And I'm trying not to, but the thing is, she keeps having them."

"Yes, I know." Mrs. Riccoli sighed.

"You do?" Elizabeth asked.

"Well, when you get woken up every night, it's hard not to notice!" Mrs. Riccoli joked. "But listen, Elizabeth, I don't want you to worry about the nightmares. I'm sure they'll stop soon."

"You are?" Elizabeth asked. She didn't feel half as confident of that somehow. "Why do you say that?"

"A couple of years ago Andrew went through the same thing, when we moved to Sacramento from Seattle. At the time I was frantic about it, but the doctor said it's not uncommon for a five-year-old to feel very uprooted. And after a few weeks the bad dreams stopped," Mrs. Riccoli explained.

"Oh." Elizabeth knew that was a rational explanation. But something about Juliana being afraid of a girl . . . what did that have to do with moving? Nothing, as far as she could tell. "That makes sense," she told Mrs. Riccoli. "And you probably know best. But Juliana always dreams about a girl— a mean, frightening girl. And that doesn't seem to have anything to do with moving."

"I know, but—who can understand the way our minds work when we're asleep?" Mrs. Riccoli shrugged. "I sure don't. Anyway, it's awfully nice of you to be so concerned. And believe me, I've got my eye on her. If you do, too, I'm sure she'll be all right."

"I guess," Elizabeth said. "Oh, before you go—I was wondering—have you seen Mr. Brangwen around tonight?"

"Hm. No, I don't think he's working tonight," Mrs. Riccoli said. "Why?"

"Well, I wanted to talk to him about something," Elizabeth explained. "But I haven't seen him. He's usually here all the time, isn't he?"

"Yes, but he doesn't have a set schedule," Mrs.

Riccoli said. "He pretty much comes and goes as he pleases. What did you need to talk to him about?"

"Oh. Well, I guess it's not that important," Elizabeth said. "Never mind." Mrs. Riccoli had enough on her mind for right now. Maybe sometime Elizabeth would suggest getting a new gardener— one who didn't scare people!

Mrs. Riccoli glanced at her watch. "I'm sorry, but I'd better run off or I'll be late for class. And if I'm late, no one's going to wait for me, that's for sure." She laughed. "See you at about nine, Elizabeth! Thanks for your concern."

"Bye!" Elizabeth called to Mrs. Riccoli as she hurried toward her car.

Elizabeth paused on the porch for a minute before going back inside the house. She looked through the window into the living room, where Juliana was working on a coloring book.

She wished she felt more comfortable with Mrs. Riccoli's explanation. But she couldn't help thinking that Juliana's problem *wasn't* the move.

If I could just find Mr. Brangwen and talk to him! she thought. She'd tell him to stop his scary stories once and for all. Then everyone could stop worrying about Juliana so much!

Winston took out the day's leftovers and put them in a glass bowl with pretty metal edges. He put it in the microwave and pressed the buttons. "On high for . . . five minutes should do it." He pressed start and watched the bowl of spaghetti turning on the carousel. He had just enough time to grab a bite to eat for dinner from the leftovers Mrs. Karsten had set out for him. He was starving!

It was seven forty-five, and the twins had dropped off to sleep just a few seconds earlier while Winston sang lullabies to them and glued things back together. Fifteen dollars wasn't nearly enough for all the work he'd done that night, in his opinion. He deserved thirty dollars at least. But he'd take twenty. That would leave him with five bucks after he gave the rest to Charlie. No problem.

He was leafing through a magazine on the counter when he heard the Karstens' car pull up in the driveway. He jumped to his feet and tried to look incredibly busy, straightening the playpen in the living room.

"Oh, hi!" he said, trying to act casual when they walked through the front door.

"Hello, Winston. We headed home a few minutes early," Mrs. Karsten said, putting her purse and several shopping bags on the kitchen table.

"Thought we'd give you a break since you filled in last minute and all. I'm sure you have plenty of homework to do," Mr. Karsten added.

"Homework? What's that?" Winston joked. "No, I took care of it this afternoon, thanks."

"Well, good. Glad to hear it," Mr. Karsten said.

"So how was the shopping? Did you buy two of everything? Because Karla and Kevin don't seem to have grasped the concept of sharing yet," Winston said. "They each tried to take half of me!"

Mr. Karsten laughed. "I know how that feels!"

"Was it OK tonight?" Mrs. Karsten asked. "Besides being pulled two ways at once?"

"Sure, it was great—" Suddenly there was a loud popping sound, as if something were crackling.

"What was that?" Mr. Karsten looked around the kitchen.

Mrs. Karsten paused in front of the microwave just as another loud buzz erupted. "It's sparking!" she cried. "It's my—my Tiffany bowl!" She stared at the microwave, horrified.

"Well, just shut it off—here, it's no problem," Mr. Karsten said, walking over to her.

"Tiffany? Who's Tiffany?" Winston asked with a nervous laugh.

All of a sudden the microwave made a loud, exploding *pop*, blowing the door open. Winston cringed. Smoke and steam billowed out of the microwave, filling the room with the smell of burnt metal and fried spaghetti. Winston wanted to crawl under the couch.

"You know . . . I'm not that hungry after all," he said, edging toward the door. "So thanks for everything and—"

"Wait a minute, Winston," Mr. Karsten said in a stern tone. "We need to talk."

Uh-oh. "We do?" Winston asked. He had a feeling this was going to be one of those "talks" where he did all the listening!

* * *

"Now, Winston. Mrs. Karsten and I have talked things over between ourselves, and we have a few things we need to discuss with you," Mr. Karsten said. He emerged from the kitchen, where he and his wife had been speaking in heated whispers for the past five minutes.

Winston's stomach was tied in knots. "Oh—OK—sure," he sputtered.

"You know how happy we've been with you so far." Mr. Karsten cleared his throat as he took a seat in the rocking chair by the fireplace.

Winston smiled uneasily, perching on the edge of the couch. He figured that the less he said at this point, the better.

"We'd like to have you back. But unless you can explain how this little accident happened, I'm afraid this will be the end of our working relationship," Mr. Karsten continued. "Do you have anything to say?"

"Um . . . well, I was in a hurry," Winston began. "See, I was so busy with the twins that I missed dinner, and then I was hungry, and—"

"But you didn't check to make sure you were using a bowl without metal in it. And this is a very serious mistake," Mr. Karsten said.

"It is?" Winston asked. Didn't everybody do that at least a couple of times in their life? Then he remembered the Karstens warning him about what he could and couldn't put in the microwave, and his saying he knew enough about microwaves to write a book. *Some book,* they were probably thinking now. *101 Ways to Bust a Microwave.* "I mean, of course, sir, it is a very serious thing to break a microwave, and I'm so sorry."

"It's not that you damaged the microwave—"

"And my Tiffany bowl," Mrs. Karsten added, clearing her throat.

Winston had a feeling she was going to hold a grudge against him for the rest of her life for ruining her bowl.

"But if you could overlook something like that— well, that doesn't give us much confidence in your abilities to safeguard Karla and Kevin." Mr. Karsten shook his head. "I'm sorry, Winston, but we can't afford any mistakes like that."

"But I'd never—I'd never do anything to put the twins in jeopardy—" Winston struggled to explain.

"Probably not. But we can't afford that risk," Mr. Karsten said. "We're sorry to have to let you go."

"Well, um, OK. I understand, I guess," Winston said politely. "So . . . I guess if you want to pay me now, I'll be on my way."

Mr. and Mrs. Karsten exchanged shocked looks.

What's the deal? Winston wondered. *Don't they want me to leave?* "Is there a problem?" he asked. "Besides the microwave?"

Mr. Karsten frowned at him. "Winston, how about if we call tonight even? You helped us out, but you also broke our microwave. We'll put the fifteen bucks toward a new one. And you're free to go—we won't ask you for any more money—"

"Even though we really should," Mrs. Karsten interrupted.

Ask for more money? Winston thought incredulously. *What are they talking about? I'd better get out of here before they make me sign an IOU!*

Winston rushed over to the door and quickly opened it. He was about to go outside when he thought . . . one last try couldn't hurt. Could it?

"So . . . there's no chance at all of me being paid for tonight?" he asked, turning around.

"Good night, Winston." Mrs. Karsten practically closed the door in his face.

Winston stood on the front stoop, staring into the dark night. Did they have to be so harsh about it? What was one little microwave compared to the loving care he'd given their kids? Now not only was he out fifteen bucks, he was out of a job.

And as far as his little secret with Charlie was concerned, he was out of excuses . . . and luck. *I might as well walk around school tomorrow with my accordion strapped to my chest!*

Or a giant note that said, "Warning! Warning! Nerd approaching!"

Nine

"Mom, you're going to love Mrs. Riccoli's house," Jessica said on Wednesday afternoon. "I can't believe you haven't been by to look at it yet!"

"Well, maybe it's because you never told me where it *was*," Mrs. Wakefield replied, turning the corner smoothly in their new minivan. "Every time I asked you about it, we got interrupted, or—"

"Well, never mind, because you're about to see it now. Take a right here," Jessica instructed. "Wow, this new car is great. There are cup holders everywhere!" She set her bottle of juice in a cup holder between the front seats. "Good choice."

"I like it, too," her mother replied. "Especially now that I know we can afford it!" Mrs. Wakefield paused at an intersection. "Right or left here?"

"Right again," Jessica said, stretching her legs. She

couldn't wait to get to Mrs. Riccoli's and start raking in the money for baby-sitting solo—that is, until Todd showed up to help her after his basketball practice. She didn't quite know how she felt about baby-sitting with Todd. She supposed she could use his help, but she'd much rather have twice the work and twice the money.

"Jessica? Is this house over on Bella Vista?" Mrs. Wakefield asked, carefully watching the road up ahead of them.

"Just off it," Jessica said. "Go around this corner and then . . . here, turn right. There it is! That huge white house up on the hill! Isn't it beautiful?"

Her mother slammed on the brakes.

"Mom! What is it—a cat? A squirrel?" Jessica tried to peer out the window.

"N-no," Mrs. Wakefield said, turning white as a sheet. "It's not . . . anything like that."

"Then what?" Jessica asked, staring at her mother.

"It's . . . that house. I—I can't go in there," Mrs. Wakefield stammered.

"Come on, Mom," Jessica said with a giggle. "Don't tell me you were taken in by all those rumors!"

"Rumors?" Her mother looked puzzled.

"Yeah! Even Elizabeth and I know that house isn't really haunted." Jessica shook her head. "Those stories about ghosts and spirits and all that—none of it's true!"

Mrs. Wakefield gripped the steering wheel tightly. "It's not that. I realized I can't . . . take that job after all. I mean—I just remembered something and I—"

"Mom, sure the place looks a little dilapidated on

the outside, and maybe it could use a fresh coat of white paint, but that's no reason to back down," Jessica argued. "Anyway, you *told* Mrs. Riccoli you'd at least take a look at it and try to help her. And she's *waiting* for us." Behind them a horn honked, and Mrs. Wakefield flinched. "Besides, we can't just stop here in the middle of the street!" Jessica reminded her.

Mrs. Wakefield nervously glanced in her rear-view mirror as a car pulled around and passed them. "I'm—I'm in the way here," she said, taking her foot off the brake. "Okay, I'll go up to the house, but I'm only dropping you off."

"Mom, chill. Even Elizabeth and I were scared the first time we came up here, and we're way more chicken than you," she teased, glancing at her mother to see if she was smiling. She wasn't. *What's up with her? Mom's turning into a nervous wreck on me!*

"Turn here," Jessica instructed, and they pulled into the driveway. She noticed that her mother's hands were shaking as she took the keys out of the ignition. "Mom? Are you feeling OK?" Jessica asked, climbing out of the minivan.

"Fine," Mrs. Wakefield said, staring at the house. "I'm . . . fine. I just didn't realize . . . I mean, I didn't realize how busy I'm going to be."

"Well, busy's good. Come *on*." Jessica practically had to drag her mother away from the car and push her onto the lawn. First her mother was afraid of the house . . . and now she was afraid of working too hard? Since when? "Look, I know you might think this is a huge job, and I know you're really busy. But don't worry about it. I can help! And I'm sure Mrs. Riccoli will understand if it takes you a little longer than you thought, because she's a very nice person."

They climbed the steps to the porch, and Jessica rang the doorbell. "I wonder where all the kids are," she mused. "They're usually rushing around, just waiting to pounce on us. It's this game they play called Ambush!" She laughed and looked at her mother, expecting her to join in.

But Mrs. Wakefield was looking anxiously around the porch and didn't seem to be paying any attention to Jessica.

Suddenly the front door swung open. "Hello, Jessica! Alice, nice to meet you." Mrs. Riccoli held out her hand for Mrs. Wakefield to shake.

But Jessica's mother didn't move an inch. "Mom!" Jessica urged. This was beginning to get embarrassing.

"I—I'm sorry, Christina," Mrs. Wakefield sputtered. "Something's come up. I'm afraid I can't help you fix up your house after all." She turned around abruptly and walked down the steps.

Jessica watched her go, completely astonished. Her mother, walk out on a client? That *never* happened! "But Mom—," Jessica began to protest.

"Mr. Wilkins will pick you and Todd up later tonight!" her mother called to her from the car. Then she closed the car door with a slam and started the engine.

"Is your mother feeling all right?" Mrs. Riccoli asked, looking completely puzzled. "She seemed awfully—upset."

Jessica watched as her mother pulled out of the driveway, driving faster than she normally would. "I don't know, Mrs. Riccoli," she said slowly, wondering what had upset her mother so much. "I really don't know."

Sundown. Why did I ever mention sundown? Winston thought as he sat on the deck at the back of his house. He rested his chin in his hands and stared at the empty lawn furniture. Now that it was dusk, it would be that much easier for Charlie to beat him up without anyone seeing or knowing.

Wait a second, Winston thought. *Charlie's not going to beat me up. That was what he threatened to do last year. This year he's going to tell everyone that I spend my Saturdays up at Mr. Pagnowski's office, playing polkas.*

Winston sighed and slumped down even farther. That was even worse than getting beat up. It was public humiliation! And he could just picture Charlie and his dumb friends, laughing at him and enjoying every second he squirmed.

All of a sudden he heard someone yelling, "Winston! Oh, Win-nie!"

Winston cringed. It was Charlie, calling out in a high-pitched singsong voice, coming to find him. The sun was sinking over the horizon, and Winston's social life was about to end.

Winston held his breath. Maybe if he stayed very, very quiet, Charlie wouldn't find him. And then what? Well, Charlie would probably call that night, lie in wait for Winston outside school tomorrow . . . harass Winston until he turned twenty-one. . . .

"Hey! Winston!" Charlie shouted.

Winston didn't move a muscle. He didn't know what he was going to do, but he hoped that if he sat there long enough, he'd think of something.

"Egghead! Are you in the garage or something?" Charlie called out. "What are you doing—building yourself another accordion?" He snickered, and his voice echoed in the empty, open garage.

Winston stood up and peeked around the corner of the house just in time to see Charlie walk into the garage. *Aha!* he thought. *Perfect!* He dashed over to the garage and, before Charlie could even see him, he closed the door and bolted it on the outside.

Winston had always hated his family's old-fashioned garage, which was the only one on the block without an automatic door opener. But now the old-style swinging door with the bolt on the outside was coming in very handy! He felt like a scientist who had just trapped a very rare bug in a box. *Thanks for being so unhip, Dad!* he thought happily.

"Winston! Was that you?" Charlie came over to the garage door and started pounding loudly on it. "Egbert, let me out of here and give me that fifteen dollars!"

Winston covered his mouth with his hand, suppressing a giggle. Maybe he could scare Charlie by making him think that the door had closed permanently on him. Winston would still somehow have to come up with the money at some point, but at least he could have fun first!

"Winston, come on. I know it's you, and I know you're out there. So quit fooling around and open the door!" Charlie yelled.

Winston leaned against the side of the garage and admired the glowing red sunset. If only he could keep Charlie trapped in there until he finished high school. But he supposed his dad would need to park the car at some point.

"Winston," Charlie said. This time his voice sounded different. He wasn't yelling anymore. "Winston, p-please," Charlie stammered. "You've got to let me out of here."

Winston didn't respond. He knew Charlie was only using that new, frightened tone to fool him. He wasn't falling for it. Did Charlie think he was born yesterday?

Then he heard it. A whimper. Followed by a sob.

Charlie? he thought. *Was that really Charlie Cashman . . . crying?*

"Please, Winston—you've got to let me out of here! I'm afraid of the dark, and I'm going crazy!" Charlie gulped through his tears.

Winston felt like running into his house to get a tape recorder. This was a moment he didn't want to forget.

Then again, he told himself, the guy was famous for wriggling out of difficult situations—like homework he hadn't done or pranks he was responsible for. He had to be faking. Well, he could whimper all he wanted. Winston wasn't budging.

"Please!" Charlie cried. "Please, Winston! No, you've—you've got to let me out—I can't—"

Maybe he's faking. But that sounds awfully real. Winston couldn't take it anymore. He hated to see or hear anyone suffering! He quickly unbolted the garage door and swung it up, letting the dusky light stream into the garage. Charlie was standing against the wall, rubbing tears from his face with the sleeve of his sweatshirt.

Wow, Winston thought. *He really wasn't faking!* "So," he said as Charlie walked out of the garage, blinking away a final tear. "You're afraid of the dark."

Charlie shrugged. "Yeah."

"Weird. Cosmic. It boggles the mind. I mean, you, Charlie Cashman, afraid of the dark! I didn't think you were afraid of anything." Winston shook his head. "Who would have guessed? Who at school would *possibly* believe that you're afraid of the dark?" A horrible, wonderful idea was slowly occurring to Winston—probably the same way an idea had occurred to Charlie as he sat in Mr. Pagnowski's office, watching Winston play the polka. Who needed the Karstens for their dumb money? Winston could use his wits to get out of this one.

"It would be pretty easy to prove," Winston said, pacing around Charlie in a circle. "Because, you know, you could easily get shut into a classroom with the lights off, or a closet, or—do you think you'd fit into a locker?"

"What do you want, Egghead?" Charlie grumbled, glancing up and down the street as if he wanted to make sure no one was listening.

"Well, I know what I just saw a minute ago," Winston said. "But I could probably forget your fear of the dark just as quickly, if, say . . . you forgot about my polka lessons?"

Charlie nodded. "OK. You win."

"Look at it this way, Charlie." Winston patted him on the back. "We *both* win."

Charlie glared at him. "Don't push your luck."

"Oh, it's not luck. It's skill," Winston said, smiling at him. "And since we're supposed to be even now, that means our little deal is off, and that means—you need to give me back that fifteen dollars." Winston held out his hand.

"I—I'll get it to you," Charlie stammered.

"When?" Winston demanded. "What time?" This put a whole new light on being a bully. Winston could suddenly see why Charlie enjoyed it so much!

"Tomorrow at school—homeroom. Now quit bugging me!" Charlie took off, hurrying away down the street.

Winston sat down on the curb and watched Charlie run. He couldn't imagine a better way to spend his evening!

Ten

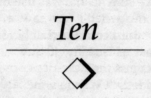

On Thursday morning Elizabeth sat down at the breakfast table and sleepily poured cereal flakes into a bowl. This late night studying had to end soon! She was the last person to get up, and she only had five minutes to eat breakfast before she left for school.

When I start sleeping later than Steven and *Jessica, there's a problem,* Elizabeth thought with a wry smile.

She took a few bites of cereal and leafed through the open newspaper on the table. She was almost too exhausted to even focus on the words. *Better snap out of it, Elizabeth,* she told herself, *or else you're going to be useless at school.*

She took a sip of orange juice and turned the front section to the last page so she could finish reading an article.

That was when she saw it. A headline. In the

obituary section. "Expert Gardener Dies." A shiver went down Elizabeth's spine.

Her eyes widened at the small snapshot of Mr. Brangwen. The photograph looked like it had been taken at least twenty years ago. "Herbert Brangwen passed away unexpectedly in his sleep on Tuesday night. He worked as a gardener for his entire life, spending his final years at the old Sullivan mansion—"

Elizabeth flipped the newspaper over, her hands shaking as she tossed it across the table. She didn't want to read any further. *Mr. Brangwen—dead. In his sleep.*

Elizabeth had a vague, creepy feeling that this had to mean something, though she had no idea what. She almost didn't *want* to know.

She pushed her chair back and ran upstairs, shivering all over.

"Jessica, I've told you a hundred times. I couldn't take the redecorating job at Mrs. Riccoli's house because I'm simply too busy!"

Jessica stared at her mother, who was chopping carrots for a salad and pretending to be calm. But Jessica knew the truth—her mother was upset about something that had to do with Mrs. Riccoli's house. And Jessica was going to get it out of her, if it took her all night!

"Mom, you weren't too busy on the way over there," she argued.

"Well, I hadn't really thought things through at

that point," Mrs. Wakefield replied, tossing the carrots into a bowl. "But when I saw the house—"

"You totally freaked out!" Jessica told her.

"I did not *freak out*, as you put it." Her mother frowned.

"Ahem." Jessica cleared her throat. "Then how do you explain how you slammed on the brakes and the fact that you wouldn't even go into the house? Wait a second!" She suddenly had an idea. Her mother *was* a lot older than her—maybe she knew something about the old Sullivan mansion! "Mom, do you *know* something about why that house was abandoned for so long—and why everyone made up all those creepy stories?"

Mrs. Wakefield stared at Jessica for a second, then shook her head vigorously. "No, of course not."

"Are you sure?" Jessica asked suspiciously.

"Yes, I'm sure," Mrs. Wakefield said.

"You're sure you don't know what happened there?" Jessica pressed. "Because from the way you freaked out, it's almost like something happened to you."

"Jessica, will you stop asking me if I'm *sure*?" Her mother sounded irritated. "I told you, I don't know anything."

"Well, you sure seemed afraid of something," Jessica remarked.

Mrs. Wakefield took a deep breath. "Well, all right. I was afraid of something," she admitted.

"Aha!" Jessica cried. "I knew I was right!"

"I was *afraid* of overextending myself and not being able to complete all the work I already promised other people," Mrs. Wakefield said briskly. "When I saw the kind of job Mrs. Riccoli needed . . . that huge Victorian mansion . . . I knew I wouldn't be able to help her."

"But Mom, if it hadn't *been* for Mrs. Riccoli, you wouldn't have those other jobs in the first place," Jessica argued, throwing up her arms, completely frustrated. "You can't just use her to get work for you and then dump her because you don't have time or think the job's too big or whatever! What if she holds it against me? What if she doesn't want *me* to baby-sit for her anymore?"

"Well." Mrs. Wakefield wiped her hands on a dish towel and put it back on the hook. "If you ask me, you guys are spending too much time working there anyway. I think you ought to consider cutting back on your hours at Mrs. Riccoli's."

"Why? Because you think the ghosts might get *us*, too?" Jessica shook her head. "Really, Mom. I just never imagined you'd be so chicken about a bunch of old rumors. My own mother, afraid of a haunted house—not that it's haunted now, because the Riccolis live there."

"I'm not afraid! And I'm not saying it again." Mrs. Wakefield sounded very irritated. "I've never been in that house, and I don't know anything about it! I just think you two need more time for your homework."

"Mm-hm. Whatever you say, Mom." Jessica watched her mother carefully as she started tossing the salad. She'd seen enough episodes of *Murder with Malice* to know that whenever someone denied something *that* strongly, something weird was going on.

And Jessica would definitely find out what it was. Somehow, some way.

"Oh, hi, Mrs. Karsten." Winston hesitated, struggling to put the phone to his ear and pull his accordion off his chest with his other hand. "How are you?" He didn't know what else he could say. Why was Mrs. Karsten calling him? Did she want the fifteen dollars he'd earned his *first* night baby-sitting back now, too, to pay for the replacement microwave?

"I'm fine, Winston!" Mrs. Karsten cheerfully greeted him. "How are you?"

"Fine, thanks," Winston said cautiously. Mrs. Karsten didn't *sound* angry, but she could just be warming up to start scolding him. "Um . . . how are Karla and Kevin doing?"

Mrs. Karsten sighed. "Well, that's why I'm calling. They're not doing very well."

"They're not?" Winston asked. "Wait—they're not sick or anything, are they?" He could just see the twins coming down with the flu and the Karstens finding some way to blame it on him. Well, he'd had his shots—he could prove it!

"Oh, no. They're not sick," Mrs. Karsten said.

"But—look, Winston, I know things ended on a rather unpleasant note the other night."

Rather unpleasant? Winston thought. *I worked like a dog for three hours without getting paid!*

"And I'm sorry if we seemed angry with you. Well, we were angry, and maybe that's why we overreacted. You see, we think we may have acted a little too quickly in dismissing you," Mrs. Karsten said. "As it turns out, the twins seem to have become very attached to you. Last night we tried a new baby-sitter. Kevin kept saying 'Win-win!' all night, and Karla wouldn't stop crying."

"Win-win? Really?" Winston blushed.

"Yes. I think the twins miss having you around," Mrs. Karsten said. "Which is why I'm calling. I wonder if we could put Tuesday night behind us and start over. Say, this Friday? Would you be available?"

"Hm." Winston pushed a key on his accordion, lying beside him on the bed. The twins were so cute . . . but the work was so hard. *We're talking about my Friday night here!* Then he remembered that these days he spent his Friday nights practicing for his Saturday accordion lesson. And it wasn't like he had a hectic dating schedule, either. Winston didn't need the money as desperately as he had before, but it would come in handy. Then again, the last time he'd helped the Karstens, they hadn't exactly come through in the financial department.

"Winston?" Mrs. Karsten asked nervously.

"I'm just thinking," Winston said.

"Oh, well . . . I have an idea!" Mrs. Karsten said. "Since we didn't end up paying you last time, how about if we double your rate for Friday night?"

Winston grinned. This was more like it! It never hurt to have some extra cash lying around, just in case Charlie got any more bright ideas. Besides, he kind of missed the twins, too.

"Mrs. Karsten, that sounds great," Winston told her. "What time do you need me? And is it OK if I bring my accordion?"

Maybe babies liked accordion music. *They* wouldn't know if it was a cool instrument or not. Besides, with the twins around, Winston would have *thirty* fingers to play it with.

He'd have to ask Mr. Pagnowski for some sheet music with lullabies.

"Well, are you sure you can't do it?" Elizabeth asked Todd on Thursday afternoon at around five, curling the telephone cord around her wrist. "Because I'm so behind in English. Mr. Bowman already gave me an extension on one poem, and I can't ask him for another."

"Elizabeth, I'd love to help you if I could. But there's no way I can baby-sit tonight," Todd said. "I just worked there last night. Besides, I had basketball practice all afternoon and my parents won't let me out of the house until I finish my science report."

"Oh." Elizabeth sighed. "Well, I already asked Winston, and he can't do it. So I guess I'll call Amy."

"I bet Amy will help you out," Todd said. "That's what best friends are for, right?" He laughed.

Elizabeth tried to smile, but she couldn't make herself. She was too worried. Ever since she'd seen that article about Mr. Brangwen dying, the thought of going back to the Riccoli mansion made her sick with fear.

Mr. Brangwen had warned her and Juliana not to close their eyes . . . and then he had died in his sleep. She tried to tell herself it was a coincidence. He was an old man, after all. His time had probably come. But part of her just didn't believe that.

"Thanks anyway," she told Todd. "See you tomorrow." She hung up the telephone, then started dialing Amy's number.

Elizabeth crossed her fingers. *Please be home, Amy. Please be able to baby-sit for me tonight.*

"Hello?" Mrs. Sutton answered.

"Oh, hi, Mrs. Sutton. It's Elizabeth. Is Amy there?"

"Hello, Elizabeth. Hang on a second," Mrs. Sutton said.

While she waited for Amy to come to the phone, Elizabeth nervously arranged and rearranged the magnets on the refrigerator. If Amy couldn't work, maybe Jessica could handle all the kids on her own. She tried to tell herself there was nothing *really* to be afraid of—but she couldn't help feeling jittery.

"Hi, Elizabeth! Sorry it took me so long," Amy said. "I was outside."

"Oh, that's OK. Listen, I was wondering if you

could do me a huge favor and baby-sit at the Riccolis tonight," Elizabeth said.

"No, I can't," Amy said. "We're having some people over for dinner. Why don't you want to go? I thought you loved working there."

"I do," Elizabeth said. "I mean . . . I did."

"So what happened? Oh—is this because of that obituary you saw this morning?" Amy asked.

"Yeah." Elizabeth sighed. She'd told Amy about Mr. Brangwen's obituary as soon as she got to school that morning. "It makes me really uneasy. I know it's stupid, but it gives me the creeps."

"Well, it is too bad about Mr. Brangwen. But Elizabeth, he was eighty-three years old, right? Dying in your sleep is a completely natural way to die when you're older. My grandfather died in his sleep, remember?" Amy asked.

"Yeah. I know," Elizabeth said. "But remember what Mr. Brangwen said to me? About never closing my eyes?"

"You told me that he said never close your eyes in that house," Amy argued. "He died at home, right? So the two things can't be *connected*, if that's what you're thinking."

Elizabeth thought it over. Amy did have a point. And Juliana hadn't had any nightmares the night before, when Jessica and Todd were there— Elizabeth had asked them both about it. "Maybe you're right. Maybe now that Mr. Brangwen's gone, he won't keep giving Juliana those scary ideas."

"Exactly!" Amy said. "That's the right attitude. The weird stuff is probably all over. And you definitely don't have anything to be afraid of. Juliana's probably been sleeping like a log now."

"I hope you're right." Elizabeth frowned.

"Well, there's only one way to find out," Amy said.

"I guess," Elizabeth admitted.

"Anyway, Jessica's going to be there with you. What do you have to be afraid of?" Amy asked. "If some creepy spirit came floating down the stairs, she'd probably tell it that its clothes were *hopelessly* outdated."

Elizabeth giggled. Maybe she *was* overreacting. Maybe she'd heard one too many scary stories about the house being haunted. Anyway, Amy was right. At the very least she needed to check on Juliana and make sure she was doing OK. "So what are spirits wearing these days, anyway?" she joked to Amy.

"Oh, the usual. Flashing lights, vapors," Amy replied.

Elizabeth laughed. There was nothing like that at the Riccolis—she was sure of it!

Eleven

"I'm going upstairs with Gretchen and Andrew," Jessica told Elizabeth Thursday night at around seven-thirty. "We're going to read some stories until they fall asleep."

Elizabeth nodded, looking up from the Chutes and Ladders game she and Juliana were playing. She could hardly believe she'd felt so afraid earlier that evening. She was having a great time at the Riccolis' with Jessica, as usual. "Sounds like a good idea. Have you checked on Nate lately?"

"Yeah, he's fast asleep," Jessica said. "And Olivia's supposed to be doing her math homework, but she's been on the phone with a friend for the last half hour."

"A girl after your own heart," Elizabeth teased.

Jessica stuck out her tongue at her twin and left the room with Gretchen and Andrew.

"Jessica *loves* to talk on the telephone," Elizabeth explained to Juliana. "She'd talk all night long if my parents would let her."

"Maybe that's what I can do," Juliana said happily. "Then I won't have to go to bed!"

Elizabeth frowned, concerned. This was exactly what she didn't want to hear! "But . . . I thought you weren't having nightmares anymore. Jessica and Todd told me you didn't have one last night."

Juliana giggled. "That's because I *fooled* them. I didn't go to sleep!"

"Not ever? Not even when your mom got home?" Elizabeth asked, putting down her game piece. *She* couldn't even stay up all night, and she was a lot older than Juliana!

Juliana shook her head, her curly brown hair flying. "Nope. And I'm not going to sleep tonight, either. That way she can't get me!"

"Juliana. You know you can't stay up forever," Elizabeth said. "That won't work."

Juliana's smile slowly faded.

"You're tired, aren't you? I know I am, and I slept at least six hours last night, which is six hours more than you slept," Elizabeth said.

"I'm almost six years old!" Juliana cried.

"I know. But I'm talking about how many *hours* you're supposed to sleep every night. To grow to be a big girl, you have to sleep eight hours a night—not zero! It's so you can be healthy," Elizabeth said.

Juliana didn't look convinced.

"Did you know," Elizabeth said, grabbing Juliana's foot, "that when you sleep, that's the only time you grow taller?"

Juliana shook her head.

"Yes, it's true," Elizabeth told her. She could remember her mother using the same line with her when she didn't want to go to bed. She'd always pictured Jessica, the marathon sleeper, growing to an incredible six feet and towering over her—that had made her jump right into bed!

"I don't care if I get bigger," Juliana protested.

This isn't working. How can I convince her to sleep? Elizabeth wondered. She had to think of a way she could make Juliana feel safe enough so that she wouldn't be afraid of bad dreams.

"I have an idea!" Elizabeth said. "I bet that if you don't sleep in your bed, you won't have those awful dreams. So why don't you sleep on the couch next to me? We can watch TV for a little while in the den, and when you're sleepy, you just drop off to sleep and I'll stay there with you, OK?" Elizabeth asked.

Juliana nodded eagerly. "I'm going to sleep on the couch! Like a grown-up! Yay! And," she added, getting up from the floor, "then I'm going to grow even taller than *Andrew*. I'm going to call *him* shrimp!"

"Go change into your pajamas and I'll meet you in the den," Elizabeth said, laughing.

Elizabeth looked down at Juliana's soft, peaceful face. She'd been sleeping soundly for the past fifteen minutes. Elizabeth figured it was safe to leave her.

She got up slowly, putting a large couch cushion where she had been sitting beside Juliana so that she could stay in the same position. *Not that she'll notice I'm gone! She's so overtired, she won't wake up until morning.* And with Mr. Brangwen no longer around to fill her head with scary images, Juliana was going to be perfectly fine from now on.

As she walked past the stairs Elizabeth could hear Andrew and Gretchen upstairs, fighting as usual, and Jessica refereeing, trying to get them to go to bed. Elizabeth smiled. The Riccoli house was really starting to feel like home.

She filled the sink with hot water and dish detergent and started washing the dishes. She scrubbed some melted cheese off the pan they'd used to make grilled cheese sandwiches for dinner, remembering how Nate had pulled his in half, stretching the cheese as far as it would go until finally it snapped. She was rinsing the frying pan when a hair-raising scream pierced the air.

Elizabeth's heart sank. Not Juliana—not again! She dropped the pan, and it clattered into the sink.

Juliana was sitting bolt upright on the couch, her eyes filled with terror. "She hurt me! She scratched me with her fingernails!"

Elizabeth rushed into the den, throwing her arms around Juliana. "It's only another bad dream, Juliana. It's OK. You don't have to worry!"

"It's not just a bad dream! It's not! She's real!" Juliana cried.

Elizabeth stroked Juliana's long brown hair. "No, she's not real—it's OK." As she held Juliana and listened to her cry, she knew that she couldn't help her anymore. And neither could Mrs. Riccoli. Juliana definitely needed to go talk to someone more experienced than she was—a doctor who helped kids get over bad dreams.

"Do you think you could try to fall asleep again?" she asked Juliana, grabbing a tissue and brushing the tears off the little girl's cheeks.

Juliana shook her head fiercely.

"OK." Elizabeth couldn't quite blame her. "My mom always gives me back rubs when I'm upset. How about a back rub? Would you like that?" she offered.

Juliana nodded, snuggling back down on the couch. She lay down on her stomach. Elizabeth moved back a bit so that she was sitting at Juliana's waist.

"OK! One superdeluxe very special Elizabeth Wakefield spa back rub coming up!" Elizabeth rubbed her palms together. "Now, don't be ticklish, or it won't work as well." She reached up to start with Juliana's neck and shoulders.

Elizabeth gasped, her fingers just inches from Juliana's skin. Her eyes widened in disbelief as she stared at Juliana's shoulders and upper arms. Her skin was completely covered with scratches! Long, deep scratches—the kind that could be made by fingernails, just like Juliana dreamed! And they were new, fresh scratches, as if they'd been made only minutes ago.

Elizabeth's eyes filled with tears. Somebody *was* trying to hurt Juliana while she slept! But why? She looked nervously around the room. Who could possibly have gotten into the den and gotten out so quickly without her hearing them?

"Elizabeth? What about my back rub?" Juliana asked, her voice muffled by the couch cushions.

"Oh—I—just a second," Elizabeth said, rubbing Juliana's lower back lightly and staring at the scratches on her shoulders. Who could possibly want to hurt Juliana? Was there really a girl waiting to get her in her sleep?

"Jessica? I can't fall asleep without Mr. Bear," Gretchen said. "Can you get him for me, *please?*" She looked up from her bed with wide, innocent eyes.

"OK," Jessica said. How could she resist anyone who looked so cute? "But as soon as I get him you've got to fall asleep, because your mom's going to be home any minute."

Gretchen nodded. "I will, I promise."

Where have I heard that before? Maybe . . . all night long? Jessica thought with a smile. Gretchen was always promising her things—and never doing them! But Jessica liked her so much, she almost didn't care.

Jessica went into the hallway. She thought she remembered Andrew throwing Mr. Bear upstairs when he and Gretchen were fighting. She glanced up the circular stairway to the third floor. She'd never been up there, but it looked kind of cool . . . even if it was dark and shadowy.

She looked at the bottom of the stairs for a light switch, but there wasn't one. So she slowly and carefully climbed the stairs to the third floor. At the top she ran her hand over the wall, searching for a light. Nothing. "Didn't they believe in light in the old days?" she complained. "I should have brought a candle." Her eyes adjusted a little, and she crept down the dusky hallway, searching for the stuffed animal. "Mr. Bear . . . oh, Mr. Bear . . . ," she called out.

All of a sudden her shoe hit something and she went flying forward, tripping and almost falling flat on her face—but she managed to catch herself by putting her hands out in front of her. Her palms slammed into the wall.

To her amazement, a thin layer of plasterboard crumbled under her hands, and she found herself staring at a hidden door. "What's this?" she whispered. A hidden door? She'd always read about things like this—but she'd never seen one before. "And a hidden door . . . always leads to a hidden room," she said under her breath.

Do you dare? a little voice inside her asked.

You're Jessica Wakefield. Of course you dare, another voice replied.

She rattled the doorknob and slowly pushed open the door, her heartbeat pounding in her ears.

She wiped a giant sticky cobweb out of the way and stepped into the room. Jessica spotted a candle beside the door, on a small table. "Not that there would be any matches—oh. There are." She picked up the large box of long matches. They looked so old-fashioned—she'd never seen matches that long before. She blew the dust off the matchbox and carefully lit the candle.

As the room brightened, Jessica's eyes widened in surprise. She was standing in a young girl's bedroom, filled with toys, dolls, and stuffed animals—the closet was full of small dresses. But the room looked as though it hadn't been used in years and years!

Dust covered everything, and Jessica sneezed a few times as she walked around, trying to figure out why the room had been boarded up and hidden for so long. There didn't seem to be anything wrong with it. So what was the big deal?

Along one wall of the room there were two windows as well as a glass door—all covered in wood. Jessica felt like she had just stepped into an old fairy tale. *What if I can't get out as easily as I got in?* she thought fearfully. She almost wondered if she should have left something to help her find her way back. Not that she expected anything to happen—it just felt weird, being in a musty room that had been locked up for so long.

She took one last walk around the room, running her fingers over the bed, the dolls, the toy chest. Then she paused in front of a large bulletin board, where a child's paintings and drawings and a couple of photographs had been posted.

Maybe I'll see a photo of the little girl who lived in this room! she thought excitedly. *Because I can't just go back downstairs and tell Elizabeth I came in here—without anything to show for it!*

She thought she heard a shriek downstairs. *I'd better hurry. Elizabeth might need my help. Just one more minute . . .* She held the candle a little closer to the bulletin board. "Aha," she whispered, zeroing in on a photo of two teenage girls with their arms around each other's shoulders. They were standing on the front porch of the house, smiling at the camera in the sunlight, wearing party dresses.

One of the girls looked oddly familiar. Jessica carefully tugged the photo off the board, gripping the tall candle tightly in her other hand. As she moved the picture closer to the candlelight she gasped. How could that little girl be . . .

She turned the picture over. On the back a child had written "Alice and Eva." Jessica's blood froze. It was true. One of those girls in the picture was a young Alice Wakefield—Jessica's mother!

She watches as the young girl with pretty blond hair enters her room. Her face burns. Nobody is supposed to be in her room! That is why it is all closed up. It is hers. Nobody else belongs here!

The blond girl walks around the room, looking at things, examining the walls. She has some nerve! the girl thinks, *watching her carefully. Looking at my things! Touching them! Who does she think she is?*

The blond girl takes her photograph off the bulletin board. She picks up the old square photograph and stares at it, and as she does her eyes grow wider, as if she recognizes somebody in the picture.

She shouldn't pick that up. She shouldn't look at it. That's mine!

That pretty blond girl has no business looking through her private room. And one thing is for sure: she is going to regret ever having invaded her secret, special place. That girl is going to be sorry.

Because she will meet with a fate worse than she can ever imagine . . .

SWEET VALLEY TWINS™

Created by FRANCINE PASCAL

Ask your bookseller for any titles you may have missed. The
Sweet Valley Twins series is published by Bantam Books.

Created by FRANCINE PASCAL

We hope you enjoyed reading this book. If you would like to receive further information about available titles in the Bantam series, just write to the address below, with your name and address:

KIM PRIOR
Bantam Books
61–63 Uxbridge Road
London W5 5SA

If you live in Australia or New Zealand and would like more information about the series, please write to:

SALLY PORTER
Transworld Publishers (Australia) Pty Ltd
15–25 Helles Avenue
Moorebank
NSW 2170
AUSTRALIA

KIRI MARTIN
Transworld Publishers (NZ) Ltd
3 William Pickering Drive
Albany
Auckland
NEW ZEALAND

All Transworld titles are available by post from:
Bookservice by Post
PO Box 29, Douglas, Isle of Man IM99 1BQ

Credit Cards accepted.
Please telephone 01624 675137 or fax 01624 670923
or Internet http://www.bookpost.co.uk
or e-mail: bookshop@enterprise.net for details.

Free postage and packing in the UK.
Overseas customers allow £1 per book (paperbacks)
and £3 per book (hardbacks)